**She chuckled**
**"You're migh**

"Only when it comes to what I want. And I want you, Lina." He reached out, his large hand cupping her cheek as he tilted her face up toward his gaze.

Her pulse quickened as the heat of his palm penetrated her skin. Once again, logic abandoned her and allowed her emotions free rein. Looking into his dark eyes, with the memories of all they'd shared passing between them, she knew it was only a matter of moments before he kissed her. And if he kissed her, it would be all over for her, as far as putting up any resistance went.

He rotated his upper body, slowly leaned in her direction.

She wet her lips with the tip of her tongue, torn between logic and desire. Could she really trust him with her heart again? Parts of her were still unsure. She needed to buy herself some time, give herself space to think this through more fully. So she blurted, "It's going to rain any minute."

Dear Reader,

Thanks so much for picking up *Every Beat of My Heart*! I sincerely hope you'll enjoy it.

What can you do when you have to choose between something you really want and something that could change your life? That's the question Rashad and Lina are facing. Only one of them can be victorious…or is that really the case?

Get ready to find out as you go on this steamy, sensual journey!

All the best,

*Kianna*

AuthorKiannaAlexander.com

# Every Beat of My Heart

## Kianna Alexander

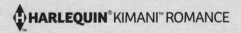

Recycling programs
for this product may
not exist in your area.

ISBN-13: 978-0-373-86456-0

Every Beat of My Heart

Copyright © 2016 by Eboni Manning

For questions and comments about the quality of this book please contact us at CustomerService@Harlequin.com.

**Printed in U.S.A.**

**Kianna Alexander**, like any good Southern belle, wears many hats: loving wife, doting mama, advice-dispensing sister and gabbing girlfriend. She's a voracious reader, an amateur seamstress and occasional painter in oils. Chocolate, American history, sweet tea and Idris Elba are a few of her favorite things. A native of the Tar Heel State, Kianna still lives there with her husband, two kids and a collection of well-loved vintage '80s Barbie dolls.

### Books by Kianna Alexander

### Harlequin Kimani Romance

*This Tender Melody*
*Every Beat of My Heart*

Visit the Author Profile page
at Harlequin.com for more titles.

For my daughter, whose inquisitive mind
sees adventure around every turn,
and whose loving heart embraces everyone she meets.

## Acknowledgments

I'd like to thank Kianna's Royal Kourt, for all their hard work in getting the word out about my books. I'd also like to thank the other Harlequin Kimani Romance authors who've embraced me as a new author to the line, making me feel like family. My appreciation is owed to my husband and children for bearing with me through the deadline doldrums. And of course, I thank each and every reader who has ever taken the time to read my work.

I'd like to salute fellow authors Rebekah Weatherspoon and K.M. Jackson for their work in increasing the visibility of diverse romance. Follow the #WOCinRomance and #WeNeedDiverseRomance hashtags on social media to add your voice.

This book heavily features the works of jazz pianist Thelonious Monk, who is considered a pioneer of the genre. I'm proud to say he was born in my home state of North Carolina. I encourage you to download or purchase Mr. Monk's work. To find out more about his life and his art, visit the following websites.

Thelonious Monk's official website: MonkZone.com

The Thelonious Monk Institute of Jazz:
MonkInstitute.org

# Chapter 1

Lina Smith-Todd breezed into her office, shutting the door behind her. Tossing her purse onto the floor next to her desk, she flopped down in her chair, a smile plastered across her face. She'd just returned from court. She had made such a compelling case for her client, she was sure the bailiff and court clerks were still talking about it. Well, at least that's what she wanted to think.

She'd been tackling cases as an employment lawyer for the Lerner Law Firm for seven years now. Through the last days of her tumultuous marriage, a contentious divorce and those early days of singlehood, she'd managed to keep her sanity by focusing on her work. Throwing all her energy into her clients' cases left her little time for pity parties.

Today's showing in court had been especially impressive. She'd say it was in her Top Five Best Arguments of her law career. Her smile broadened as she recalled the flustered look on the face of Ray Deocampo, her opposing counsel. She hummed to herself as she booted up her computer, preparing to tackle her exploding inbox.

The phone on the top of her black lacquer desk started ringing before the email program had a chance to fully load. Typing with one hand, she grabbed the receiver and used her shoulder to hold it to her ear. "Hello?"

"Ms. Smith-Todd, I'd like to see you in my office." The voice on the other end of the line belonged to Gwendolyn Lerner, the owner and executive partner of the firm.

"I'll be there in just a moment." Replacing the receiver in the cradle, Lina stood. She knew better than to enter her boss's office with a victory grin, so she went to the small wardrobe that occupied a corner of her office. Opening the door, she looked at herself in the mirror, adjusting her expression from full tilt gloating to something pleasant, but professional. Satisfied, she left her office and headed down the hallway to see what Mrs. Lerner wanted.

She found Gwendolyn's office door slightly ajar, and let herself in. Gwendolyn, dressed impeccably as always, today in a charcoal-gray skirt suit and matching pumps, looked up upon her entrance.

Lina watched her boss in silence, observing her manner and expression. Gwendolyn Lerner was an amazing litigator and very personable. At times, she could also be a hard-ass. Generally, one could tell if Mrs. Lerner was in a good mood or not within about thirty seconds of stepping into her office.

With a smile, Gwendolyn set aside the stack of paperwork she'd been reading and gestured to one of the empty chairs in front of her large cherrywood desk. "Please, Lina, have a seat."

Relieved to see that Gwen seemed to be in good spirits, Lina slid into the chair. "You wanted to see me, ma'am?"

"Yes, and thank you for coming over so promptly." Gwen leaned back in her chair, tenting her fingertips.

Lina smiled in response, curious as to what her boss would say next.

"I wanted to congratulate you on your argument in court today. Apparently it was very convincing, because I just received a call from the court saying that opposing counsel has dropped their case."

Before she could stop herself, Lina gave a few triumphant fist pumps. But once she remembered where she was, she tempered her reaction a bit. "That's great news."

"Don't stop celebrating on my account. You've earned it. And there's something else you've earned."

Lina's ears perked up, and she shifted her body, sitting forward in her chair. Could this be it, the moment she'd dreamed of since she'd first come to Lerner Law as a lowly legal assistant?

"You've done impressive work for Lerner Law, from the very first day you arrived. You've shown yourself to be more than competent, and I think you're ready for the next step."

Lina was now on the edge of her seat, hanging on Gwen's every word like a kid holding an ice cream cone on a hot day. It had taken her almost five years to make junior partner. Could she really be moving up so soon after her last promotion?

Gwen seemed to be enjoying drawing this out.

But the suspense was killing Lina.

Finally, mercifully, the smiling executive attorney said the words Lina had longed to hear ever since she'd watched her first episode of *The Practice*.

"I'd like to make you a senior partner in the firm."

It took all Lina had to hold back the squeal of delight rising in her throat. She stood to shake her boss's hand as the response she'd begun practicing the day she graduated law school fell from her lips. "I'm honored, ma'am, and I accept. I'll do my best to live up to your expectations."

Gwen smiled and released her hand. "I don't doubt that for a second."

Lina watched as her boss sat back down, then followed suit. She was so giddy on the inside that keeping a straight face was becoming difficult. The moment she got back to her office, she knew she would be busting a celebratory move. It would probably be the Running Man, or the Butterfly. Hell, she was so excited, she might even have to throw in the Cabbage Patch.

Gwen's voice broke into her thoughts. "It will take a few weeks to finalize things. Since I'm also going to offer Tara Mitchell a senior partner position, I'm going to go ahead and order new signage for the office, stationery and all that. Of course, I'll talk to finance about adjusting your salary to reflect your raise in pay."

Lina knew she was probably smiling too hard, but she couldn't help it. "Thank you. Thank you so much, Mrs. Lerner, for having faith in me."

"Call me Gwen. After all, before long, we're going to be Lerner, Mitchell and Smith-Todd."

Hearing that gave Lina pause. It had been four years since she'd divorced her ex-husband, Warren. Yet she still used his name to hyphenate her own, as if she were still married to the cheating asshole. She'd been so busy with climbing the ladder of success that she'd never gotten around to having it changed. Now that her name was about to be on the building, she sure as hell wasn't going to be identified by the last name of a man she could barely stand to be around.

"Smith. Lerner, Mitchell and Smith. If my name's going up in lights, I want it to be my name, not Warren's."

"Sounds like I just gave you the motivation you needed to go and get your name legally changed."

Lina stood. "You sure did. Is there anything else you need from me?"

Gwen shook her head. "No, that's all for now. I'll have a contract drawn up for you to sign in a few days. In the meantime, it looks like you've won yourself some time off, since the Reedy case was dropped. So I'll see you Monday."

With a wave, Lina departed and went back to her own office.

Inside the glass walled room, she closed all the blinds on the wall facing the corridor. Then, when she was sure none of her colleagues could see her, she kicked off her pumps and performed a Running Man move that would have put any *Soul Train* dancer to shame.

The pinging of her email program, which was open and running on her computer, grabbed her attention. She shimmied over to the desk and took a seat. There, on the screen, was a calendar reminder she'd set for herself several weeks ago. Reading the text, she grinned.

She'd seen an article a while back on a social media site announcing an upcoming auction. After reading the article, she'd set the reminder because there was an item scheduled to be sold that she just had to have: a piano played by the legendary Thelonious Monk.

The auction would take place tomorrow night, and the timing couldn't be better. Between her savings and the substantial raise she'd soon be getting as Lerner Law's newest senior partner, she would be in a position to make a competitive bid on the piano. And when she got her hands on it, she planned to have it delivered straight to her mother, Carla.

Carla had been in poor spirits lately, as age and stress had conspired to cause her health to decline. But Lina knew that owning the piano played by her very favorite musician would do wonders on raising her mother's spirits. Lina had been treated to Monk's music from the cradle. She didn't know anyone who appreciated Monk's artistry the way her mother did.

*Except for Rashad*, her traitorous thoughts reminded her.

She sighed as she thought of her ex-flame. He'd been in her life for only a few weeks before she'd become unable to put up with his secretive ways. As a woman who'd already endured the humiliation of a cheating spouse and a failed marriage, she craved transparency and openness. Rashad had seemed unable, or unwilling, to provide that, so she'd walked away from him. And just as she always did when her personal life went awry, she'd thrown herself into her work. Only this time, her immersion in work had paid off in a big way.

Pushing aside thoughts of Rashad and his tight-lipped behavior, she began gathering her things. A three-day weekend in early June was a rare treat, and she intended to enjoy it. She'd kick back for the rest of the evening, then spend her Friday planning the perfect strategy for winning the bidding and securing Monk's piano for his biggest fan: her mama.

Once she'd packed up, she grabbed her phone and purse and strode out the door.

Rashad MacRae ran a hand over his face, stopping at his mouth to stifle a yawn. A glance at the wall clock hanging across from him showed that it was eleven minutes past six. He should have left the courthouse over an hour ago. Summertime meant an increase in marriages, and as an assistant register of deeds for Mecklenburg County, the influx of paperwork always landed on his desk.

Stamping his name on the last few pieces of paper

needing his approval, he stood from behind his desk and stretched his arms above his head, hoping to ease the tightness in his shoulders. He strode across the room to the single-cup coffeemaker he kept atop a bookcase and set it to make a cup. The way he was feeling, he would need the jolt of java to keep him awake for his commute home.

While the coffee brewed, he filed away the papers he'd been working on and searched around for the day's edition of the *Charlotte Observer*. He'd picked up a copy at lunch, and even though he couldn't see it amid the clutter on his desktop, he knew it was there somewhere. After a bit of straightening up, he still couldn't find it.

He got his coffee, added a bit of sugar and sat back down at his desk. The first sip of the dark brew seemed to jump-start his memory, and he recalled where he'd stashed the newspaper. Opening the top drawer of his desk, he pulled it out. While he drank his coffee, he skimmed the front page. A small headline in the bottom right corner caught his attention.

King's Guitar, Monk's Piano, Among Items to be Auctioned This Week. See Article, p. 6A.

His eyes widened. Monk's piano. Surely they didn't mean… He quickly opened the paper to page 6A to read the article. Sure enough, the piano in question had once been played by Thelonious Monk, Mr. "'Round Midnight" himself.

A smile spread across Rashad's face. As a young

musician, he'd looked up to Thelonious Monk, study-ing his style and recordings almost religiously. It was Monk's artistry that first inspired him to put his hands to those eighty-eight keys. So owning a piano once played by the master himself would be a lifelong dream come true. He knew the piano would cost a pretty penny, but one couldn't really put a price tag on a piece of musical history as significant as this.

He pulled out his smartphone and opened the notes app, keying in the details of the location, time and date of the auction. As he did, he realized that the auction would be held the very next evening. Once he had the information saved to his phone, he tucked it away. Fold-ing the newspaper, he went to tuck it back into the top drawer of his desk.

As he slid the drawer open, the smiling face of a woman looked up at him.

He lifted the photograph from the drawer and held it up.

It had been taken last fall at his friend Darius's wed-ding. It was of Lina looking gorgeous in her brides-maid's dress, smiling brightly for the camera. Behind her, he stood with his arms looped around her waist.

They'd broken up months ago, but he hadn't been able to part with the photo. She had looked so care-free, they both did. That day, they'd just started to ex-plore what their mutual attraction could lead to. And it had led to plenty: plenty kisses, plenty smiles and plenty of good lovemaking. He'd started to fall for her, started to think about the possibility of becoming a one-woman man.

Then her mistrust had reared its ugly head, derailing their relationship before it really had a chance to get established. She assumed that because he didn't volunteer every mundane detail of his life, he was hiding something from her. She didn't seem to understand that he just wasn't one for discussing things in that way. She'd demanded to know everything about him, but he hadn't been ready to reveal so much of himself. So she'd dropped him, walked away without a backward glance.

What she didn't know was that he'd never stopped thinking about her. She might have given up on their relationship, but he hadn't. He'd stopped calling her once he realized she wasn't going to speak to him, but he knew he'd get another shot. Charlotte was a large city, but not so large they wouldn't eventually run into each other. And when they did, he intended for her to hear him out, just one more time. If she still didn't want to see him, then so be it. But he had to try because deep inside, he knew she couldn't resist the molten-hot physical attraction that had drawn them together in the first place.

Smiling, he tucked away the newspaper and the photo. Lina was out there somewhere, and he would square things away with her soon enough. Right now, he had another mission.

Come tomorrow night that piano was going to be his, and he didn't care how much it cost.

## Chapter 2

Lina arrived at the one-story building housing Cleveland and Wendell Auction House around four on Friday afternoon, a full two hours before the auction was set to begin. She wanted to make sure she got a good seat up front, where the auctioneer could easily see her paddle.

There were many items up for sale at that night's event, including paintings, antique furniture and even a few other musical instruments connected to some important person or another. Despite the impressive array, she was only interested in one thing: Monk's piano.

She'd chosen a black sheath and a pair of matching pumps for the evening. The dress was long, with a slit for ease of movement. She tightened her gray wrap around her shoulders to shield herself from the subzero air-conditioning as she went to the front desk to sign in and obtain her paddle.

After securing her paddle, she moved through the well-appointed corridor toward the suite where the auction would be held. The place had an aristocratic feel due to the decor; cream-colored wallpaper imprinted with a gold brocade pattern, dark maple furniture that looked more like artwork than something to sit on. The windows were covered by velvet drapes the color of eggplants, and the floors were covered with thick Berber carpet in the same shade. Side tables held dramatic floral arrangements of tall white calla lilies in gold vases, ceramic figurines and crystal dishes displaying wax fruit.

She entered the suite and found it was decorated in the same fashion. The room had been arranged with rows of chairs much less fancy than the ones in the lobby, but still plush and cushioned. A center aisle had been created to separate the seats into two sections. All the chairs faced a raised platform in the front of the room where a podium and microphone were set up. There was no one else there, and that made her smile. As the first to arrive she had her pick of seats, so she moved toward one on the front row of the left section, bordering the aisle.

She was just about to ease her behind onto the thick burgundy cushion when she heard a male voice.

"Lina, is that you?"

She recognized the deep timbre of it right away, and her eyes slid shut. She straightened and turned slowly toward the voice, all the while willing her instincts to be wrong.

They were not.

When she opened her eyes, she saw Rashad standing at the back of the room near the door she'd just come through.

He looked so handsome he threatened to take her breath away. He wore a coal-black suit with a soft blue shirt and black-and-blue-striped tie. The suit was cut to fit his tall, muscular frame, and was well complemented by the black wing tips on his feet.

Her eyes traveled up to his face, and to the thing about him that had always made her knees go weak: his hair. The impeccably maintained dreadlocks he wore were wound and bound low on his neck. But since she'd spent many a night running her hands through his hair, she knew it was long enough to reach the middle of his back. God, he was sexy.

While she sat there on the verge of drooling, he steadily moved closer to her.

He spoke again, his voice cutting into her fantasy. "It is you. It's good to see you again, Lina."

"I...uh... It's good to see you, too." She stammered the response, disarmed by his striking good looks and easy manner.

He smiled, his soft, full lips spreading to reveal his perfect pearl-white teeth. "This is so funny. I haven't seen you in months, and this is the first place I run into you. What brings you here?"

She blinked several times as she struggled to remember why she'd come, or even where she was. What was it about this man that made her brain function slow down to a crawl?

He regarded her for a few silent moments as if waiting for her to answer his question.

Realizing she would never be able to answer him while looking at all his sexiness, she shut her eyes. That seemed to kick her brain back into gear, because she was finally able to respond. "I want to buy the piano."

"Monk's piano?"

She nodded, opened her eyes. "I don't think there are any other pianos up for sale."

He released a low, sexy chuckle. "Looks like we're after the same thing, then."

She drew in a deep breath. She knew from her time with Rashad that he loved Thelonious Monk just as much as her mother did, if not more. She'd been so focused on getting the piano, she hadn't even thought about the chance he might know about the auction and make an appearance.

He strolled up the aisle, taking the seat opposite her in the right section. His manner was as maddeningly casual as always.

Not knowing what else to do or say, she sat down. There was still a good hour or so until the auction would begin. In the meantime, she fished around in her handbag and pulled out her phone. Generally she considered it gauche to use a phone in a setting like this, but she'd do just about anything to avoid looking at the painfully handsome man seated across from her.

She was scrolling through her Twitter feed when she

sensed someone else entering the room. She looked up, swiveled her head.

Walking up the aisle was a short, ebony-skinned elderly woman. Attired in a green pantsuit, matching flats and an abundance of shimmering gold jewelry, she leaned on a pearl-handled cane as she made her way toward the front.

Rashad stood and offered his arm. "Let me help you to your seat, Mrs.…."

The woman offered a soft smile as she accepted his assistance. "Parker. Julianne Parker. Thank you, young man."

Once Mrs. Parker was seated a couple of chairs to the right of Rashad, she leaned her cane against the next seat.

Lina kept her gaze on her phone as Mrs. Parker chatted with Rashad. She could hear snippets of their conversation, and it seemed Mrs. Parker was also there for the piano. Lina sighed under her breath. Just how many people would she be competing against to get the damn piano, anyway?

The room began to fill with people as the start of the auction drew nearer. As seats around her began to fill, Lina set her phone to vibrate and tucked it away. Looking around the room, she took in the faces of the other bidders. She had no way of knowing how many of them would also be going after the piano.

The sound of Rashad's humming invaded her thoughts. Hearing that throaty sound reminded her of how well he could sing. Truth be told, the brother could blow. He had a killer tenor that reminded her of a cross between Luther Vandross and Miguel—the kind of voice that made a woman's panties just fall off. She could clearly recall the late nights he'd serenaded her as she lay in his strong arms.

She glanced over at him, and he flashed one of his unforgettable megawatt grins in her direction.

She sank down into her chair.

It was going to be a long night.

Rashad glanced across the aisle at Lina, who looked as if she wanted to disappear. She seemed uncomfortable with running into him; he, on the other hand, was thrilled to see her. He'd been all set to come here tonight and put all his focus on winning the bid for the piano. Having her here simply meant he could accomplish two goals at the same time.

She was gorgeous in the figure-hugging sleeveless dress she wore. The slit up the side was parted now, allowing him a full view of her long, beautiful bronze legs. She sat demurely, legs crossed like any good belle would do. Her short-cropped hair was carefully coiffed and curled into the edgy style that framed her lovely angular face so perfectly. She wore very little makeup, and as always, his eyes were drawn to the shiny, plum-colored lip gloss she favored.

He could clearly recall the slightly sweet flavor of that lip gloss from the last time he'd kissed her. That had been months ago. Far too long for his tastes. The longer he looked at her, the more his groin tightened with desire. There was something about the way she carried herself that drove him mad with wanting. Now that she was here, sharing the same space with him, he wanted her just as badly as he wanted Monk's piano.

What if he could have them both, make them both his in one night? Wouldn't that be something?

In his mind's eye, he saw himself sitting on the bench, in front of the grand piano, his hands poised above the keys. On top of the polished lacquer surface of the piano's top, he saw Lina. Dressed in a teal sequined dress that barely grazed the tops of her shapely thighs, she lay on her stomach, facing him. The swell of her breasts threatening to spill out of the dress, she fixed him with a come-hither stare that set his blood on fire. Her round hips and shapely long legs, capped by a pair of sexy heels, drew his appreciative gaze. She was seduction personified. A woman so fiery and passionate that she put all others to shame.

The auctioneer appeared behind the oak podium, and banged a gavel. The loud thumping pulled Rashad out of his fantasyland and back into the present. Shaking off the remnants of his daydream, he grabbed his paddle from the empty seat next to him and turned his attention to the front of the room.

It soon became obvious that Monk's piano would not be the first item to be sold. Rashad sat through the bidding on various paintings, furniture pieces and antiques, wondering when they would finally get around to it. Mrs. Parker placed and won a few bids, but he found he couldn't muster any excitement for any of the other pieces. All the while, he stole glances at Lina, who seemed just as disinterested in the other items as he was.

"Now, we'd like to offer this embellished baby grand piano, played by the great musician Thelonious Monk early on in his career. The piano comes to us from the estate of a personal friend of Mr. Monk's. We're told Henry Minton gave it as a birthday gift to Mr. Monk. Henry owned Minton's Playhouse in Harlem, where Monk developed his signature style as a member of the house band in the 1940s. The piano is gold embellished and was imported from Italy. It is in top condition, and is a rare find. We'll open the bidding at ten thousand dollars."

Rashad raised his paddle, and saw several others in the room go up, including those of Lina and Mrs. Parker.

"Do I hear ten thousand five hundred?"

More of the same.

"Eleven? Eleven thousand, five hundred? Twelve thousand…"

Rashad kept up with the lightning pace of the bidding, raising his paddle at every bid. As the dollar amount rose, the number of bidders began to drop off. By the time the auctioneer reached fifteen thousand, the only three paddles remained raised were Lina's, Mrs. Parker's and his own.

The three of them continued the bidding at a breakneck pace, passing seventeen thousand, then eighteen thousand, and then nineteen thousand dollars.

Before Rashad could raise his paddle to bid twenty-one thousand, however, Mrs. Parker grabbed the handle of her cane and got to her feet.

Her brown eyes flashing, the older woman called out a bid. "Twenty-five thousand."

On the other side of the aisle, Lina countered. "Twenty-seven thousand, five hundred."

Rashad stood. "Thirty thousand."

A short, narrow man in a blue suit stepped up onto the stage, holding a piece of paper in his hand. He passed the paper to the auctioneer, who then said into the microphone, "Excuse me a moment."

Rashad waited in silence with the others as the auctioneer read the note.

The auctioneer spoke again. "We have a call-in bid of forty thousand dollars on the table from an anonymous bidder."

Mrs. Parker raised her paddle as if she meant to make another offer, but the auctioneer stopped her.

"I'm sorry, ma'am. We've gone well over the time allotted for this item, and we have many others to get to. We'll verify the call-in bid, and if it can't be secured, we'll resume bidding on the piano tomorrow evening."

Rashad dropped into his seat, groaning. Either he'd just lost the piano, or he'd have to do this all over again tomorrow night. Whatever the case, things had not gone as he'd wanted them to.

He looked across to Lina, and saw her gathering her purse. While he might not have gotten Monk's piano, there was nothing stopping him from talking to her before she left.

He watched her walk down the center aisle and out the door in the back of the room, then followed her.

In the hallway, she turned her head and saw him, but didn't stop walking.

He didn't stop, either, and he followed her out the door of the auction house and into the muggy evening air.

The sun was hanging low, but had not yet set. She stopped by the driver's side door of her car and turned to him. "Rashad, why are you following me?"

He smiled in response to the pointed question. "I think the answer to that is pretty obvious, baby."

She rolled her eyes and opened the car door. Flinging her wrap off and tossing it into the passenger seat, she snapped back, "Don't call me baby."

"I'll call you whatever you want me to. All I ask is that you hear me out, just for a moment."

Her frown softened just a bit. She stepped away from him, moving so that the opened driver-side door of her car was between them. "What is it?"

He locked eyes with her. "I want another chance with you."

# Chapter 3

Lina could feel her heart pounding in her chest like thunder. She blinked, sucked in a breath. But that only served to fill her nostrils with the woodsy, masculine scent of Rashad's cologne. A shiver went through her body as she recalled the way that scent had smelled, clinging to her skin and to her bedding.

She raised her gaze and found him watching her in silence. Every bit of good sense she possessed abandoned her as she looked into his dark eyes. He was entirely too much man, and she couldn't help but be mesmerized by him.

His soft lips parted. "Have a drink with me. I know a little place not far from here. You can follow me there, what do you say?"

Before she could think, the response fell out of her

mouth. "Yes." The moment she heard herself say it, she cringed, knowing it was too late to take it back.

He was already striding away, toward his pickup truck parked a few spaces away. "Great. I'll drive slowly so you won't lose me in downtown traffic."

Resigning herself to go along with him as agreed, she climbed into her car, closed the door and buckled up. By the time she started the engine, he was already idling at the curb, ready to pull out into the road. She eased her car up behind his big truck and waited.

It took about ten minutes to arrive at the "little place" he'd spoken of, a bar called Shout Down Babylon. He parked in an empty spot right in front of the entrance, and she slipped into one a few spots over. By the time she'd unbuckled her belt, he opened her door and extended his hand to help her out of the car.

She took his offered hand and climbed out. Once her vehicle was secured, she followed him inside the small, one-story brick building.

The interior of the bar was smoky, as she'd expected. She could tell from the pungent scent that most of the people inside were smoking cigars or pipes instead of cigarettes. The wood paneled walls were covered with neon signs advertising beers and liquor, as well as a few battered license plates and sporting equipment. Among the artifacts were several photos of Bob Marley, Sean Paul, Mad Lion and various other performers of reggae, dancehall and soca music. One sign in particular caught her attention. She read the sign aloud. "Welcome to Bull Country. Warning: Bears Shot on Sight." Shaking her head at the old athletic rivalry between two local universities, she raised herself onto one of the padded leather stools.

Rashad simply sat next to her, at his towering six foot two inches of height he didn't need to stretch or stand on his toes to sit on a bar stool. As the bartender approached, he ordered a root beer.

When the bartender turned to her, Lina said, "I'll have a ginger ale with lemon, please." She knew better than to drink alcohol. It was hard enough for her to resist Rashad while sober. The last thing she needed right now was to make a stupid mistake with him, one she couldn't take back.

With his bottle of root beer in hand, he asked casually, "How have you been?"

She offered a soft smile. "Pretty good. Actually, I just found out yesterday that I made senior partner at the firm."

His easy grin broadened, his eyes lighting up as if to express his genuine happiness. "That's great, congratulations! I know you've wanted that partner spot for a long time."

She felt the blush creeping into her cheeks as he raised his bottle in her direction. She remembered the talks they'd had during their brief time as a couple. While he hadn't been very forthcoming with details of his life, she'd openly shared her hopes and dreams with him.

He took a long draw from his bottle.

She squirted lemon into her soda and sipped from her own glass, noticing the awkward silence that had fallen between them. To break it up, she asked, "How about you? What have you been up to since I last saw you?"

He set the bottle down, his eyes connecting with hers. "You mean, other than thinking about you?"

She sighed, rolling her eyes.

He seemed to take the hint, and altered his approach. "I've been doing fine. I still work for the register of deeds office, still do the Wednesday night shows with the band, though we did take a little hiatus while Darius and Eve were on their honeymoon."

She smiled at the mention of her best friend and her new husband. "These days, she's glowing. It's the happiest I've seen her in a long time."

"Darius is certainly happy, it even shows through in his playing on stage. Speaking of the shows, I haven't seen you at one in a while."

She lowered her gaze from his. "I think you know why, Rashad."

He frowned. "Not really."

She folded her arms over her chest. "You're kidding, right?"

"I know you and I aren't together anymore."

*Because of your secrecy*, she wanted to say. But she held her tongue and tried to keep the annoyance off her face.

"You can still come and enjoy the music."

Rolling her eyes again, she met his gaze, and instantly regretted it. There it was again, that look he was so good at giving her. The dark, coffee-colored pools of his eyes seemed to hold a mixture of sincerity and desire. The longer she stared, the more she felt herself falling into them, being dragged back into his world.

The electronic jukebox behind her suddenly started up, blasting Shaggy's hit "It Wasn't Me." The pounding syncopation of the music snatched her right out of Rashad's world and back into reality. Shaking off the remnants of his charms, she decided to use this evening to her advantage. "So, how bad do you really want Monk's piano?"

His back stiffened, as if he didn't like that she'd changed the subject. "I'm sure I want it more than you do. You've never been into Monk the way I am."

She cocked an eyebrow. "True, but my mother is about as big a fan of Thelonious Monk as a person can be."

Now his brow hitched in surprise. "You mean you want the piano for your mother?"

She nodded. "She's been feeling poorly lately, and I know she'd love to have it. It's just the thing to raise her spirits, and since I got the promotion, I figured, what the hell?"

He cupped his chin, moving his fingers along his smooth, clean shaven skin. "That's honorable and everything, and no offense to Mrs. Smith, but I'm going to do whatever I have to, to win the bid."

"Is that so?"

"Yes. I hope your mother's health improves, but we're talking about a piece of jazz history here. If it wasn't for Monk, I never would have touched the eighty-eights. I *have* to have this piano."

She couldn't hold back her chuckle. She had nothing

but respect for civil servants, since she worked with them on a daily basis. However, she also knew they weren't exactly well paid. "You and I aren't the only ones who want it, and from the looks of Mrs. Parker, she's got some serious resources."

He shifted on the bar stool, downed the last of his root beer. His gaze hardened and focused on the wall of spirits behind the bar. "You don't think I can beat her bid?"

"No offense, but it's a possibility. She looks like she could outbid us both."

"Speak for yourself. You don't know everything about me."

She scoffed. "That's for damn sure."

He swiveled his head toward her. "Are we really going to do this here? Do we really need to revisit your trust issues?"

She pursed her lips. "My trust issues? I'm not the one who always had something to hide."

"Not telling you every single detail of my life is not the same as hiding things from you."

Draining the last of her ginger ale, she grabbed her purse and slid from the bar stool. "That's where we disagree, Rashad. I opened up to you, and all I got in return was the brush-off."

"I'm not your ex, Lina. You're never going to be happy until you stop blaming all men for his shit."

That did it. She turned her back on him, and without anther word or a backward glance, strode to the door and left.

\* \* \*

Rashad dunked a boneless buffalo wing into his cup of ranch dressing and popped it into his mouth. From his corner of the booth at the Brash Bull, he had a pretty good view of the big screens displaying various sporting events. The televisions were muted, as usual, with the closed-captioning turned on. Most of the noise in the place was coming from the booth he shared with the other members of his jazz quartet, the Queen City Gents.

The men were currently entertaining themselves by teasing Darius about his so-called honeymoon glow. Having returned less than a month ago from an island hideaway with his new bride, Eve, Darius's personality had taken a noticeable turn toward sappy.

Darius, the band's bassist and Rashad's ace since their days in college, pounded his fist on the table. "Y'all are just jealous that I'm getting some on a regular basis, and from a gorgeous woman at that."

Swallowing a mouthful of beer, Marco scoffed. "Please. I never lack for female affection." The saxophonist, a native of Costa Rica and a self-proclaimed ladies' man, wore an expression that conveyed just how sure of himself he was.

Darius groaned. "Marco, we're not talking about man-whoring. We're talking about commitment here."

Ken "the Zen" Yamada, the band's drummer, barely looked up from his phone as he spoke. "This is why I don't bother with dating. Women are just a source of contention between us."

Darius shot back. "You know, Ken, I'm starting to think your ass is gay."

Rashad simply smiled at their banter, preferring to enjoy his wings and beer instead of get involved in their pointless debate.

From his seat on the bench, Darius elbowed Rashad. "Don't you have something to say, man?"

Rashad shook his head, keeping his eyes on the television nearest the table. "Nope. Not a damn thing."

He was watching the local twenty-four-hour news channel focused on happenings around North Carolina. An image of two wrecked cars appeared, and Rashad read the transcript ticking by on the screen.

As he focused on the news anchor's words, he realized that the accident had taken place in Charlotte, and that the owner of the auction house he'd been at last night, as well as the auctioneer, had been injured. The story continued to scroll by, ending with an announcement that the auction house would be closed, and all auctions would be postponed for at least two weeks.

"What are you staring at, Rashad?" The question came from Marco, and cut into his thoughts.

"The news. It looks like I'll have to wait for my shot at Monk's piano. The auction house is shut down for a couple of weeks." Rashad grabbed a napkin and wiped the wing sauce from his fingers. He'd been looking forward to going over to the auction house that night, though it wasn't his usual Saturday night activity.

Now, with the auction delayed, he could put more of his focus on obtaining the other rare treasure he wanted to make his own: Lina.

He imagined how she would act in a courtroom, arguing some poor opposing counsel under the table; or in her office, diligently attending to client paperwork and phone calls. She took her career very seriously, and he didn't blame her. Her passion for the law was evident, and as the old saying went, if you do what you love, you'll never work a day in your life.

Darius elbowed him in the ribs. "Rashad, I hear there's drama at county. What do you know about it?"

Darius's pointed question drew Rashad out of his fantasy, and he groaned. "All I know is that the county budget is being cut, drastically. Right now, we don't know how it's going to affect us at the courthouse."

"Sounds like things are pretty uncertain over there." Marco ran his hand over his chin as if thinking.

Rashad agreed. "They are. What about you, how are things in the fast-paced financial world?"

"Same old, same old." Marco shrugged, as if his work as vice president of Royal Community Bank was no big deal.

Rashad knew better. Royal was the largest minority owned private financial institution in the state.

Ken volunteered, "I'm in the running for a pretty big design contract for the city. Hopefully the budget cuts won't put the kibosh on it."

Rashad doubted the budget cuts would cause problems for Ken. As a skilled graphic designer, Ken's services were always in demand. Aside from that, it was almost always more economical to hire a freelancer than to take on the costs of a full-fledged employee.

Darius joked, "No one ever asks me about my work."

Rashad shook his head, punched his friend in the shoulder. "That's because we all know you don't do any. As long as you keep inviting us down to the beach house, we're willing to overlook it."

"Don't be jealous of my awesome retirement."

Rashad scoffed and punched him again. "Don't be an ass about it, then."

The basket of wings in the center of the table was empty now, so Rashad used a couple of Wet-Naps to clean up. Grabbing his wallet from the back pocket of his black slacks, he pulled out a twenty to cover his share of the tab and tip.

"I'm out, guys." Rashad eased out of the booth, keys in hand.

His friends said their goodbyes as he strolled out of the building.

Inside the cab of his pickup truck, he started the engine and pulled out of the small lot. He thought about Lina as he navigated the streets of downtown Charlotte, taking I-77 out of the city toward his luxury housing complex.

The way she'd walked out on him the previous night, he knew he should probably let her cool off. Since he'd obviously upset her, he was willing to give her some space. Still, he was not willing to walk away from her, and what they could have together.

She was such a cynic, and he understood why. According to Lina, her ex-husband, Warren, had been an asshole of the highest order. He'd cheated on her at every opportunity and then further insulted her by assuming she was too stupid to figure out what he was up to. Any woman would be cautious after what she'd gone through.

What Rashad didn't understand was why she insisted on making him bear the burden of her mistrust. Sure, he flirted with the women in the front row when the Gents put on their shows, that was part of the act. He was lead singer, and if smiling and winking at a few women kept ticket sales up, what was the harm in that? Somehow, Lina had associated his stage persona with his true self, and assumed that if he winked and charmed from the stage, he must be seeing other women behind her back.

That couldn't be further from the truth. When they were together he'd been faithful to her. Hell, since he'd broken up with her, he'd been on a self-imposed hiatus from dating and sex. After Lina, no other woman seemed to capture his interest.

By the time he pulled his truck into the two-car garage beneath his unit, he'd made up his mind. He'd back off for now, give her a few days to be mad at him. But come next week, he fully intended to ask her out again, so they could heal the rift between them.

A woman like Lina was as rare and precious a find as Monk's piano, and he didn't intend to let either slip through his fingers.

## Chapter 4

By Monday morning, Lina had managed to push most of her annoyance at Rashad aside, in favor of working on a new case. He hadn't contacted her over the weekend, and she was glad. She was about to embark on a new phase in her career as an attorney, and the last thing she needed right now was to be distracted. Rashad MacRae was about the biggest distraction she'd ever encountered.

She shifted through the case files on her desk, looking for a particular piece of paperwork she needed to get started on her research. After a few moments of flipping through the pile, she realized she wasn't getting anywhere. She pressed a button on her intercom system and asked her legal assistant to come in.

Randi Mayer entered a few moments later, the long

strap of an attaché case slung over her shoulder. She was professionally dressed as usual, wearing a soft blue button-down shirt with a pair of navy blue boot-cut slacks. She also wore a pair of navy pumps with heels so high Lina wondered how she kept from twisting her ankles with every step. The young woman, a recent graduate of Duke Law, was extremely efficient at her job. If anybody could find what Lina needed, it was Randi.

"Are you looking for the Needleman files?" Randi asked the question as she crossed the room toward Lina's desk.

Lina rubbed a hand over her forehead. "Yes. Do you know where they are?"

Randi extended a manila folder. "Here they are. I took them yesterday afternoon, typed them up and made copies. I should have told you, but by the time I finished, you'd already gone home for the day. Sorry about that."

Relief caused Lina's breath to escape in a long sigh. "Thanks, Randi." Now that she had the files in her possession, she could get on with the rest of her day. As she flipped through the neatly typewritten pages, she thanked her lucky stars for such an efficient assistant.

"Do you need me for anything else?" Randi stood by the desk, waiting.

Knowing how tiresome it must be to stand in one place in those sky-high heels, Lina gestured to one of the two empty chairs on that side of the desk. "Yes. Go ahead and have a seat. With any luck, we can finish up our pretrial preparation before the day is out."

Randi sat, pulling out a yellow legal pad and pen from her case. She crossed her legs and grasped the pen. "Okay, Ms. Smith-Todd, I'm ready."

Opening the case file to the first page, Lina began dictating. "Case file for case number 26008, Howard Needleman versus Dewey and Fowler Incorporated."

Lina then began to speak about the particulars of the case while Randi transcribed. Howard Needleman claimed to have been unfairly targeted by his new boss. Mr. Needleman insisted that his new superior, Kate Miller, was a female chauvinist who'd placed him on probation for no other reason than to threaten his job. At first, Lina had thought the case far-fetched, but Mr. Needleman and a few of the other men working in his office had presented her with compelling evidence to support his claims.

While Howard remained the only named plaintiff, four other men working in middle management within Dewey and Fowler all had similar stories. Two had been placed on the same kind of employment probation as Howard, and the other two spoke of several negative encounters with Mrs. Miller. One man had even taken it upon himself to use his smartphone to record audio of one of Mrs. Miller's tirades. The Needleman case was, by far, the most interesting one she'd ever been tasked with.

As lunchtime approached, Lina's bleary eyes and growling stomach made her close the case file. "Let's take lunch, I'm starved."

Randi ceased her writing and put away her pad and pen. "See you back here in forty-five?"

Lina smiled. "Tell you what. We've both worked so hard this morning, let's make it an even hour."

With a giggle and a wave, Randi left the office, closing the door behind her.

Pulling a tissue from the box sitting on her desk, Lina dabbed at her tired, watery eyes, careful not to disturb her eye makeup. She frequently ordered lunch from the deli a few doors down from the firm. They had great sandwiches and their proximity meant her lunch was always delivered in twenty minutes or less. Today, though, she'd been sitting in one place for so long she decided to walk down there and pick up her lunch herself, hoping the physical activity and fresh air would give her a second wind.

A few minutes later, she was strolling along Morehead Street, enjoying the early summer sunshine. The kelly green sleeveless sheath she wore was perfect for the weather, leaving her arms and legs exposed to keep her from overheating in the warm, slightly humid air. She'd left her cream-colored cardigan in the office—while she needed it to fight off the chill of the air-conditioning inside, she certainly didn't need it out here.

As she grabbed the door handle of Rhino Market and Deli, the vibration of her cell phone in her purse caught her attention. She swung the door open and stepped into the cool interior of the deli, and then fished the phone out of her bag.

"Hello?"

"Hello, Lina."

She pursed her lips, having recognized Rashad's voice right away. Chastising herself for answering without looking at the screen to see who was calling her, she replied tersely, "Yes, Rashad?"

"You don't sound happy to hear from me. Are you working through your lunch break?"

She rolled her eyes. "No, but that doesn't mean I have time to talk to you."

"Ouch. I know you're mad, and I'm sorry if you were offended the other night."

She went to the red plastic roll dispensing numbers and pulled one, noting how Rashad had succeeded at placing the blame for what happened squarely on her shoulders. "Well, you know how crazy and unreasonable we women can be."

He was silent for a moment, as if carefully choosing his next words. "Lina, you're not going to scare me off by being snappy. There's something special between us, and we both know it."

She eased into the line. There were only two people ahead of her, and she didn't want to get into this with him now. "I guess you know about all the auctions at Cleveland and Wendell being postponed."

The sound of his deep chuckle reverberated in her ear. "Yes I know about it, and I know you're trying to change the subject."

She let her eyes sweep over the menu board, even though she already knew what she planned to order. "I'm not talking to you about this right now, Rashad."

"I'm fine with that. Let me take you out to dinner tonight, and we'll iron it out then."

The line moved as the first person in front of her

left with their food. "You're not going to let this go, are you?"

"Nope."

She closed her eyes briefly. Rashad was a charmer, always had been. It only took one night of watching him flirt with the female fans at a Gents show to see that. His ego told him that no woman could resist him, and while she'd love to take him down a peg, the truth of the matter was she couldn't resist him, either. "What time are you picking me up?"

"Seven thirty. Thank you for agreeing, Lina."

"You didn't give me much choice."

He chuckled again. "I'll see you tonight."

She disconnected the call just as her number came up. Shaking her head, she tucked the phone away and ordered her usual, a ham and Swiss wrap and baked chips.

With her food and a bottle of water, she left the deli for the walk back to her office. With every step, the dreadlocked hotness that was Rashad MacRae dominated her thoughts.

Rashad slowed his truck, his speed dropping below the twenty-five-mile-per-hour speed limit, as he neared Lina's house on a quiet residential street. Her house was in the west Charlotte neighborhood of Wilmore. The area, located several miles from the hustle and bustle of the city center, was known for being diverse, family friendly and filled with eclectic charm. He rarely ventured to this neighborhood, preferring to live closer to the action and to his work in the city. Though, for someone as focused as Lina, he could see the appeal of living there.

He eased into a spot directly in front of her house. The large ranch-style structure had soft yellow siding, with multicolored stone surrounding the pitched roof at the doorway. The neatly trimmed yard was free of flowers, but there were a few bushes bordering the front of the house. To his mind, the home was very much reflective of the owner: beautiful and appealing, without any extraneous enhancements.

He got out of his truck, straightening his tie as he walked toward the door. He'd chosen to put on one of his best gray suits, minus the sport coat to keep him from bursting into flames in the Carolina summer heat. He hoped she'd approve of the charcoal-colored slacks, lavender button-down shirt, and purple-and-silver-striped tie he'd worn with his favorite gray-and-black wing tips. Sticking to the sidewalk to avoid trampling her grass, he made his way up to the house.

He raised his fist, gave a few sharp raps on the dark stained surface of her front door. Moments later, she swung it open.

As he took in the sight of her, he swore his heart skipped several beats. She was wearing a soft green sleeveless jumpsuit. He'd encountered these things before. He and the other guys in the band had jokingly referred to them as "adult onesies." While he'd seen women wearing them on television and all over the Queen city, he'd never seen a woman who he thought looked good in one.

Until now.

The jumpsuit was made of a magical fabric that clung to every peak and valley of Lina's curvaceous body. The low cut V-neck in the front gave him a glimpse of her cleavage. Figure-grazing fabric embraced her flat stomach and her round hips and thighs, and then flared out into a wide leg over her gold pumps.

"Hi, Rashad."

Her voice snapped him out of his trance, and he realized he'd better stop ogling her so openly. His gaze drifted up to her face, taking in the barely there makeup and perfectly coiffed hair. "Lina. You look fantastic."

Her sparkling raspberry lips tilted up into a smile, then parted. "Thank you. I could tell you liked the outfit by the look on your face."

He smiled. What could he say to that? She'd caught him staring, and he couldn't say he was sorry. She looked too damn good not to stare at. The reality was, she looked good enough to eat. He'd had the honor of tasting her before, and as his appreciative eyes raked over her once more, he hoped he'd have the honor again.

She turned away from him to lock her front door.

His eyes landed on the curvy roundness of her ass, and he shut his eyes briefly as the blood filled his manhood.

She faced him again, tossed her keys into her small handbag. "Ready?"

Oh, he was ready, all right, but in a totally different sense than she meant. Deciding to keep the thought to himself, he grasped her hand and led her to his truck.

Once they were settled inside the cab and buckled in, he started the engine and pulled away from the curb.

The enclosed space of the truck's cab subjected him to the sweet, floral aroma of her perfume. Her fragrance was so feminine and intoxicating he had to take shallower breaths to keep his focus on driving. He considered turning off the air conditioner and opening the windows, but it was too muggy a night for that. She didn't say much in the car, seeming content to entertain her own thoughts while she watched the passing scenery through the passenger window. Picking up on her cues, he didn't press her to converse. There would be plenty of time for that over dinner.

Once he eased the truck into a space at the Black Rose Inn, he cut the engine and went around to her side to open the door for her. In the time it took him to round the truck's front bumper, she'd already swung the passenger door open. She was of average height, but his super-duty pickup was high enough off the ground that she might have to make a small leap to get out. He reached his hand out just in time to help her step down from the running board. Linking arms with her he escorted her inside.

The interior of the Black Rose was quiet, in keeping with the romantic atmosphere. The walls, covered in black brocade wallpaper, were decorated with framed photographic images of various rose varieties. A plush beige carpet was emblazoned with hundreds of black roses, alternating with loose petals. The round tables were cloaked in white cloths, and due to the absence of music being piped in, the only sounds were the few muted conversations being carried on by the patrons.

At the black lacquer podium near the door, Rashad gave his last name to the tuxedoed maître d', who lead them to a secluded table near a window. Once they were seated and alone, Rashad looked across the table at Lina. She had opened the menu. Her shiny pink lips flexed slightly as she silently evaluated the choices.

He could watch her all night, but decided to try to choose his meal before the waiter arrived.

When the white-coated waiter arrived, Lina ordered the citrus glazed salmon and a green salad. Rashad placed his order for the medallions of beef with herb potatoes and zucchini gratin. Rashad kept quiet until the waiter deposited their glasses of iced tea on the table and departed.

He locked eyes with the beautiful woman sitting across from him and asked the question he'd wanted to ask since he ran into her that night at Cleveland and Wendell. "Why do you really want Monk's piano?"

Her perfectly arched left brow hitched up a few centimeters. "What do you mean?"

"I mean, do you really want it for your mother?"

She nodded, the kind of slow nod you gave someone when you didn't think they were following you. "Yes, I really want it for my mother, I told you that."

He chose to ignore the insult of her slow nod, and shrugged. "I was just asking. I'm sure you know how valuable the piano is. It could bring in a lot of money on the open market."

She pursed her lips. "I don't really care about that,

I make good money as it is. When I said I wanted it for my mother, that's exactly what I meant. Once she has it, she can do whatever she wants with it. But she's much too big a fan of Monk's to sell it."

Now he gave a slow nod of his own. "All right, then."

She narrowed her eyes. "What about you? How do I know you wouldn't resell it if you won the bidding?"

He leaned back in his chair, struck a nonchalant pose. "We both know I would never let Monk's piano go, not for any amount of money."

She folded her arms over her chest. The gesture blocked his view of her cleavage, and he immediately felt deprived. "To be honest, Rashad, I don't really know you that well at all."

He knew that remark was meant to cut him. More than anything it irritated him. "Really, Lina? This again?"

Her expression was as blank and disinterested as he'd ever seen it. "Truth hurts."

Before he could line up a response, the waiter returned with their meals. The man set the steaming hot plates before them and strolled away. Rashad looked across the table at Lina, who seemed to be completely focused on her salmon. To give her time to cool off, he started in on his own food.

When he'd finished the last bite of his dinner, he set his silverware down. She was still eating, but he couldn't hold back what he needed to say to her any longer. "Lina, I'm sorry."

She paused, a forkful of salad hanging in midair.

Her golden eyes widened and her gaze locked with his. "What?"

"I said I'm sorry. For not being open enough with you when we dated, and for whatever I said or did to offend you after the fact. I'm sorry." Getting the words out was unpleasant to say the least, but certainly not any worse than the many days and nights he'd spent thinking about her since they parted ways. He'd tried everything short of apologizing to her up until this moment, and he still wasn't positive he'd done anything wrong per se. Still, if this was what it was going to take to convince her that their relationship deserved another try, then so be it.

She blinked a few times, setting her fork down. Her expression serious, she asked, "Do you mean that, Rashad?"

He nodded. "Yes. I know I'll have to work to win you all over again, but believe me, I'm willing."

Her expression softened into a Mona Lisa–like smile. "Then we'd better go somewhere more private to talk."

He grinned, not needing to be told twice. He'd finally penetrated her rigid exterior, and he planned to make the best use of his newfound access. Raising his hand, he signaled for the waiter to bring the check.

# Chapter 5

Strolling alongside Rashad through Romare Bearden Park, Lina had to admit she enjoyed his company. The feeling of his large hand cradling hers was familiar, comforting and much more arousing than she'd anticipated.

A quick glance at her wristwatch showed her that it was a few minutes past ten. The night air was warm, but thankfully less humid than it had been earlier. A soft breeze blew, rustling the needles of the towering pines and spreading the heady fragrance of their sap.

She looked over at him walking next to her, his profile illuminated the soft glow of the streetlamps lighting the path. He was well dressed tonight as usual. His sense of style was one of the things that had originally attracted her to him. She liked the colors he wore, and thought they complemented each other well. His dreadlocks, secured in a ponytail at his nape, cascaded down his back like a dark waterfall, leading her eyes to the welcome sight of his backside in the well-tailored gray slacks. She could clearly recall gripping that very backside as he stroked her to orgasmic bliss, and as the memories washed over her, she could feel the heat filling her neck and face.

"Are we going to talk now? We've been walking for a while."

His question captured her attention and pulled her out of her erotic memories. Chastising herself for the direction of her thoughts, she nodded. "Sorry, yes. I really do want to talk."

He offered up a dazzling smile. "I'm glad. Otherwise I'd just be making laps around the park in wing tips for no good reason."

She chuckled. She'd spent so long being angry with him and avoiding him, she'd forgotten how witty he could be. When he'd waltzed into Cleveland and Wendell the previous week, she hadn't been happy to see him at all. Now, alone with him under the pine trees, she could feel that initial attraction she'd felt for him when they met last year rising again. "I never said it inside the restaurant, but I accept your apology."

"Glad to hear it." He gave her hand a gentle squeeze.

"As much as I hate to admit it, you were right when you made that remark about me holding all men responsible for what Warren did to me." The bitter memories of her ex-husband's blatant and repeated infidelity had changed the way she interacted with other men.

Logically, she knew how unreasonable her disdain for men was; not all of them were like Warren. But logic rarely won out when it came to her emotions.

She glanced at Rashad, and found his eyes on her. A soft smile touched the corners of his lips.

"It wasn't meant as an insult, Lina. I just wanted you to see things from my perspective."

She nodded, their gazes still locked. Their steps slowed as they came near a wrought iron bench with its back resting against the trunk of a willow tree. With a gentle tug, he led her beneath the cascading canopy of leaves, and they sat side by side on the seat.

He draped his arm around her shoulder, and she didn't protest. Instead she inched closer to him, letting their thighs touch.

She inhaled deeply, taking in the scents of his cologne, the recently trimmed grass and the hints of the coming rainstorm hanging on the night air. "Every other man who's approached me lately has been put off by my attitude, you know."

He shrugged. "None of them could handle you anyway, if that's all it took to run them off."

She chuckled, shaking her head. "You're mighty persistent, aren't you?"

"Only when it comes to what I want. And I want you, Lina." He reached out, his large hand cupping her cheek as he tilted her face up toward his gaze.

Her pulse quickened as the heat of his palm penetrated her skin. Once again, logic abandoned her and allowed her emotions free reign. Looking into his dark eyes, with the memories of all they'd shared passing between them, she knew it was only a matter of moments before he kissed her. And if he kissed her, it would be all over for her as far as putting up any resistance went.

He rotated his upper body, slowly leaned in her direction.

She wet her lips with the tip of her tongue, torn between logic and desire. Could she really trust him with her heart again? Parts of her were still unsure. She needed to buy herself some time, give herself space to think this through more fully. So she blurted, "It's going to rain any minute."

He smiled, but didn't halt his approach. "I don't give a damn."

Before another moment could pass, his full, soft lips touched hers. As soon as their lips met, her insides melted and all thoughts of resistance drained away. Her hands moved of their own accord and gripped the solid muscled planes of his forearms, while he placed his free hand on the small of her back. The tip of his tongue darted between her lips, and a soft groan escaped her. Damn, he was as good a kisser as she remembered, maybe even better.

The first few drops of rain that hit them were ignored as the kiss deepened. The low hanging branches of the willow tree provided some degree of shelter, but as the droplets came heavier and faster, pelting her skin even through the canopy of leaves, she was dragged back to reality. She broke the seal of their lips, easing away from him.

Over the sound of the rain, he said, "I'd better get you home before we're both soaked."

She nodded, brushing away the droplets of water from her upper body.

He stood, and after taking off her heels, she followed suit. The two of them clasped hands, and dashed from under the tree. Out in the open, she laughed aloud as they ran down the footpath, sidestepping puddles. Her bare feet slid over the wet grass, but she felt confident she wouldn't fall with Rashad's strong hand locked around hers. By the time they made it back to his truck that was parallel parked on the curb, both of them were soaked to the skin.

He opened the passenger side door, and she tossed her shoes into the floorboard next to her purse before climbing in. Once she was secure in the leather seat, he walked around to the other side and slid behind the wheel.

She knew she must look a mess, and a glance in the rearview mirror confirmed it. Her formerly coiffed hair was now dripping wet, the curl returning to her flat-ironed tresses. "Sorry about getting your seats all wet."

He started the engine, pulled away from the curb. "Don't worry about it. I just wish I'd remembered my umbrella." He reached between the seats into the back of the truck's cab and showed her the long black umbrella laying on the backseat.

She chuckled. "Me, too. I left mine in the stand by my front door. Walked right past it." A chill passed over her dampened skin, and she shivered.

As if sensing that she was cold, he turned on the heat, letting the warm air flow into the cabin. "I'll admit wanting you to be wet tonight, but not like this."

In that moment she swore the temperature climbed twenty degrees. Words failed her as she looked at his profile. His full attention was on driving, so he didn't look her way, but she sensed the honesty and desire in his words. Another shiver ran down her spine, and this time, it had nothing to do with the damp clothing clinging to her body.

They rode in silence to her house. Once there, he pulled into her driveway and got out, taking his umbrella with him. By the time he opened the door for her to get out, he'd opened the umbrella. The rain had slowed a bit, but was still coming down. With the wide canopy sheltering both of them from the rain, he walked her to the door.

Clutching her shoes and handbag in one hand, she used the other to unlock her door. The lock turned and she pushed the door open, tossing her things inside the door. Turning to him, she looked up into his eyes. "Are we really going to do this again, Rashad?"

"If you'll have me, Lina. I want you, and I'll do whatever it takes to prove I'm worthy of you." The shadow of the umbrella canopy hung over his face, but she could clearly see the sincerity in his eyes.

"We have to take things slow." *I don't want to get hurt again*, she added silently.

He reached for her, letting his fingertips trace her jawline. "Whatever you want, baby." He leaned down and there, beneath the umbrella, with the summer rain falling around them, kissed her so solidly that she trembled.

When he broke the kiss and stepped back, she exhaled her pent-up breath.

"Go on inside and get out of this rain. I'll call you. Good night." He took a few backward steps, then turned and strode back to his truck.

"Good night," came her soft reply. She went inside, closing the door behind her. From the front window, she watched him pull off and drive away.

Then she sat on the sofa, watching the night rain for a long time.

Tuesday morning Rashad was elbow deep in a stack of paperwork on his desk when Gary Hall strode into his office. As far as bosses went, Gary was pretty laid-back most of the time, especially considering his position as head register of deeds. But as Rashad looked up and caught Gary's eye, he knew this morning would be different. He could easily read the anxiety on Gary's face.

Loosening his yellow paisley tie, Gary slid into the seat on the opposite side of Rashad's desk and blew out a breath.

In the awkward silence that followed, Rashad took in his boss's demeanor. His slumped posture, along with the defeated expression on his bearded face let Rashad know that something was about to go down.

Finally, Gary inhaled, and spoke. "I've got something to tell you, Mac, and I wanted to tell you in private, before the staff meeting."

Rashad rested his elbows on his desk, lacing his fingertips together. "Sure. What's up?"

Another sigh. "I just got word from the county manager's office that the operating budget has been cut."

"Again?" Rashad rolled his eyes. This was the third round of cuts in the past fourteen months.

"Yes, again. And unfortunately, this time, we're going to have to make some sacrifices in the ROD office." Gary's gaze dropped.

Rashad knew what was coming. It was the last thing he wanted to hear, but he sensed the negative vibe hanging in the air. "Who, Gary?"

The fabric of Gary's brown suit wrinkled as he shrugged his wide shoulders. "I don't know yet."

He said the words his boss didn't want to say. "But someone is about to lose their job, right?"

A slow nod was the response.

"Do we at least know how many people we'll have to cut?"

Gary's brow furrowed. "At least two, five at most, depending on their pay grade."

Rashad couldn't hold back his frustrated groan. The folks in the register of deeds office were some of the hardest-working people in county government. Due to the nature of their work, they handled tons of paperwork, and had more interaction with the county's citizens than most other staffers. That meant dealing with a lot of rude, irate folks. People who waited until the last minute to file important documents, or who came to the courthouse without proper identification to retrieve documents they'd requested. Now, some of these good, diligent employees were about to lose their livelihood. And with the economy being what it was, the timing was awful.

Gary spoke up. "There's one more thing. I won't be able to attend the staff meeting this morning, my mother-in-law is going in for hip surgery in two hours and I have to be there."

Rashad knew that Gary was a widower, and he respected his decision to take over his mother-in-law's care after the death of his wife. "Oh, yeah, that is today. I hope Harriet's surgery goes well, man.

"Thanks. Unfortunately, that means…" Gary let his words trail off.

*Shit.* "You want me to announce the cuts to the staff?"

"Sorry, Mac. With Kaye out on vacation and me at the hospital with Harriet, you're the only one left to do it."

Rashad groaned again, trailing an open hand over his face. It had been bad enough knowing about the cuts, but to have to be the one to break the news? *Shit!*

Gary looked at his leather wristwatch. "I've got to get over to the hospital so I can see Harriet before she's sedated. Again, I'm sorry about this, but there's no way around it."

Rashad nodded. "I understand, Gary. Give Harriet my best, and let me know when she's out of surgery, okay?"

"I will." Gary got up, brushed the wrinkles from his brown slacks and exited, closing the door behind him.

As the quiet settled over his office, Rashad leaned

back in his chair and tried to work out the best way to tell his staff what was coming.

Less than an hour later, Rashad was standing at the head of the table in the office conference room, looking around at the faces of his colleagues. They had been through every other item on the morning's agenda, and there was no way of putting off the announcement any longer. Straightening his black-and-silver tie, Rashad cleared his throat.

"Okay, folks. We've covered a lot of ground this morning and I want to thank you all for your co-operation. Now I have to make an announcement, and frankly, the news isn't all that good."

Claudia, single mother of three girls and one-woman office rumor mill, raised her hand.

Rashad acknowledged her.

"Is this about the job cuts here in the office?"

A murmur of hushed conversation swept over the room.

Rashad's eyes narrowed a bit, but he was somewhat relieved to have the pressure of making the announcement alleviated. "Yes, and how did you know about that, Claudia?"

Nonchalant as ever about her nosiness, she shrugged. "I was filing papers right outside your office this morning when Gary went in. He didn't close your door all the way, so I...overheard."

*You mean, you eavesdropped.* Rashad held back his snicker. "Well, the cat's out of the bag now. I'm just finding out about this myself, so I don't have a lot of information for you. All I know is that the cuts were deep this round, and we're going to lose between two and five staffers here in ROD."

The conversations in the room started up again, this time a bit louder. Rashad let the staff members talk amongst themselves for a few moments, knowing they needed some time to process the news.

Rick Havens, a twenty-seven-year veteran of the office, raised his hand. "When is this going to happen?"

Rashad looked the older man in the eye. "I wish I knew, but I don't. I expect it will be pretty soon, though."

Rick nodded slowly, a worried expression on his face.

Rashad clapped his hands together to get everyone's attention. "All right, I think I've held you up long enough for the day. Meeting adjourned."

As the staff members began to file out, Rashad gathered his briefcase and tucked his phone into the hip pocket of his slacks. Looking up he noticed Rick Havens still seated at the other end of the table. The older man looked stricken.

Rashad moved nearer to where he sat. "Rick, you okay?"

He shook his head slowly. "I'm in the number, I just know it."

Rashad placed a hand on his stooped shoulder. "Now, Rick, don't jump to conclusions. We really don't know anything yet."

His expression blank, Rick continued. "Oh, we know something. We know the county has been trying to force me to retire for the last two years, and this will be the perfect excuse to get rid of me."

With the palm of his hand still resting on Rick, Rashad could feel the tension in the older man's shoulder. "I'll do whatever I can to look out for you, Rick." And he meant it.

"I know you will, Mac. They just don't understand my situation. I'd love to retire, but I need my salary to take care of my grandkids. They don't have anybody else right now and until their aunt graduates college, I'm all they've got."

Rashad's only response was a solemn nod. He knew Rick's story. Four years ago, Rick's oldest daughter and son-in-law had been killed in a car accident, leaving him to take care of his two grandchildren. The two little boys were seven and nine, still very young. Rick's younger daughter was expected to take over the care of the boys, but she still had three semesters left of college before she earned her bachelor's degree.

Rick rose from his seat. "If you can do anything to help me, Mac, anything at all, I'd be so grateful."

Rashad walked him to the door of the conference room. "I promise to try my best, Rick. But, right now, try not to worry about it, okay?"

Rick nodded, then turned and disappeared down the narrow corridor.

Standing in the door of the conference room, Rashad watched him go. Then, with his heart heavy, he began the long walk back to his own office. All the while wondering what he could do for Rick, and the other members of his staff who couldn't afford to lose their jobs.

## Chapter 6

Lina sat next to her mother on the old sage-colored sofa Tuesday evening, rifling through a stack of appointment notices. Every two weeks, Lina came to her mother's small house to help her sort through her appointments and organize her medicines.

Carla used the tip of her index finger to push her red-rimmed glasses up on the bridge of her nose. "How are things going at work, baby?"

Lina smiled. No matter how old she got her mother still thought of her as her baby. "Great. We're still making preparations for me to start my senior partnership, and we've won two cases over the last couple of weeks."

Carla's lips turned up into a bright smile. "Senior partner. I'm so proud of you, Lina."

She couldn't help smiling back. "Thanks, Mama."

For a few moments, silence fell between them as Carla dropped her pills into the compartments of a plastic pill sorter, and Lina jotted down appointment dates in the notebook they kept solely for that purpose. Lina reflected on her days growing up in this house with her mother and her late father, Bradford. He'd been a serious man, and about as old-fashioned as they came. Still, Lina had loved her father dearly. The twelve years since his passing had softened the pain of losing him, but she doubted the sting would ever fully go away.

Closing the lid on the pill sorter, Carla set it aside. "I miss my Brad. Can't believe it's been twelve years since he left here."

She could sense the shared pain flowing between them. Bradford had died of aggressive late-stage prostate cancer, with only months between his diagnosis and his death. "I miss him, too, Mama. Sometimes I wonder what he would say about my life now."

"I think he'd be proud of you, in his own way. Even though you haven't traveled the path he preferred, there's no denying your accomplishments, baby."

A smile lifted the corners of Lina's mouth. She remembered her father as a man who had a very clear idea of the roles of men and women, one that no amount of reasoning could change. She imagined he'd be disappointed that she was almost thirty-five and still single, because he'd always placed emphasis on marriage and family.

Her eyes holding a wistful, faraway gaze, Carla broke the silence. "Your father was so set in his ways.

I guess it's to be expected, he was eleven years older than me. Yes, my Bradford was a 'my way or the highway' man."

She nodded, agreeing with her mother's words. Her father's tenure in the army as a captain had left him with a hard exterior manner. On the inside, though, he'd remained loving and fiercely protective of his wife and only daughter.

"I was nineteen when we married. I knew nothing about life, and your father was thirty years old, and had already done ten years in the service. He promised me he'd take care of me, and that I'd never have to work a day in my life. Kept his promise, too. But he was so stubborn, sometimes I wanted to box his ears."

Lina closed the notebook and set the pen aside. "All he wanted for me was to settle down with a soldier and do the army-wife thing. I don't know if I could have deviated much further from that."

"I know. Here you are single and practicing law, of all things. Your father had his ideas of what was men's work and what was women's work, and I know he thought lawyers ought to be men. Still, I saw this coming."

She cocked an eyebrow. "Really, Mama?"

"Sure I did. You were always involved in politics in middle and high school. You were class president in your junior and senior years. And remember the way you used to dominate on debate team? Nobody ever wanted to go up against Long-Winded Lina."

She chuckled, amused that her mother remembered all that. She had been a force of nature during debates, known to argue a point until her opponents gave in. Once, she'd argued so passionately in favor of allowing girls on the football team that her opponent had conceded, on the condition that she stop talking. "You're pretty perceptive, Mama."

"Maybe so. Or maybe I'm just more open-minded than your father was."

Lina knew her mother was probably right. Even though her father had attended her debates, he'd likely never considered her talents could be put to use in the workforce. Her thoughts drifted to Rashad, and she wondered what he might be up to today.

"So, tell me about your date with Rashad. Are you two back on good terms?"

"Yes, Mama. I think we are. We had a lovely time, other than getting caught in the rain." She recalled the exhilarating feeling of running through the downpour to get back to his truck, and the sweet warmth of his kiss. The memories made her heart flutter, and if she were honest with herself, she couldn't wait to see him again.

"That's good to hear. You know I'm happy so long as you are."

Lina draped her arm around her mother's shoulders and gave her a squeeze. "Thanks. I appreciate your attitude about this. My friends are always complaining to me about their meddling mothers, but you never do that to me." *And Monk's piano will be the perfect gift to thank you for being a wonderful mother.* When it came time for the bidding, Lina was determined to get the piano for her mother, even if it put a dent in her IRA.

Carla's responding smile was soft. "You know me. I've got my own life to attend to, and I'm not hurting for grandchildren. I know you'll settle down and give them to me when the time comes."

She kissed her mother's smooth brown cheek. One of the things she loved most about her mother was her laid-back manner. At sixty-one, Carla wasn't sitting around the house knitting and waiting to have grandchildren bestowed on her; she went out and lived her life. She had book club meetings, wine tastings, played golf and bridge. Her active lifestyle kept her in shape, and helped to ease some of the ailments that came with her age.

"Do any of your prescriptions need refilling?"

Carla shook her head. "Not just yet. I'll need more glucosamine pretty soon, though."

Lina nodded, tapping a note into her smartphone to remind herself to pick up a bottle of the joint supplement. While her mother took a good number of pills, only three were prescriptions, to treat hypertension, diabetes and nerve pain. All the other pills were vitamins and supplements to help her energy level and overall health.

"I think I'm squared away, baby. Go on home and get some sleep. Senior partners need their rest." Carla winked at her daughter.

Lina gave her mother another kiss on the cheek before rising from her seat. Grabbing her keys, purse and phone, she strolled toward the door. "Bye, Mama. I'll call you tomorrow."

Remote control in hand, her mother turned on the

wall-mounted television over the fireplace. "Good-night, baby."

Leaving her mother to enjoy her nightly sitcoms, Lina opened the front door and slipped out into the night.

Rashad took a moment to make sure his locks were secured at his nape before grasping the door handle of the restaurant and walking in. The place was packed, as it usually was during the lunch hour on Wednes-days. Its downtown location made it a popular mid-day stop for employees of the many businesses and government agencies located nearby. Inhaling deeply the scents of garlic and oregano in the air, he scanned the interior for Lina.

Navigating around the crowd of people waiting for to-go orders at the counter, he wove his way farther into the restaurant, still searching for her. Finally he spotted her, sitting at a two-person table in the corner. The table's location was a prime one, right in front of the large window looking out on the street. A smile stretched the corners of his mouth as he took in the sight of her.

She sat on the chair facing him, but she hadn't yet looked up from the magazine she was reading. Her shapely body, draped in a sunny yellow sheath dress, was perched demurely on the edge of the seat. Her long legs were crossed in front of her. The strappy high heels on her feet matched the dress and set off her bronze skin tone. She looked gorgeous, and he wondered how the male lawyers who argued against her in court managed to concentrate.

He made his way to the table and touched her bare shoulder. "Hey, beautiful."

She looked up from the magazine, gifting him with a bright smile. "Hey, yourself."

He angled her face a bit more to his liking with his hand, and placed a soft kiss on her lips. Moving away before he was tempted to do more, he grasped the back of the empty chair and pulled it out. As he took his seat, he asked, "How long have you been here?"

She glanced at her gold wristwatch. "About thirty minutes. I know how crowded it gets here, so I took an early lunch to get us a good table."

"Good thinking. Thanks for doing that."

"No problem." She gestured to the open magazine. "Besides, I've been trying to get a minute to read this issue for over a week now."

He watched her as she spoke, taking in the sight of her glossy, berry-colored lips. Lips he wanted to kiss again. His desire for her warmed his blood, and he reached to his throat to loosen his tie and let some of the heat building inside him escape.

"How are things at the courthouse?" She closed the magazine and tucked it into her purse.

"We're still waiting for word from the higher-ups at county about the cutbacks, so things are a little tense. Other than that, it's business as usual."

The waitress, wearing a uniform of a black skirt, white blouse and red-and-white-checked apron, approached the table. "Welcome, what can I get you?"

Lina ordered first. "I'll have the eggplant parmesan lunch special and a lemonade, please."

The waitress turned to him. "And you, sir?"

"I'll have the—"

Before he could finish his order, the waitress's eyes went so wide and round they resembled two full moons. She squealed, and then shouted, "Aren't you Rashad MacRae? From the Queen City Gents?"

He cleared his throat, a little taken aback by her excitement. He stuck out his hand, as he usually did when a fan of the band approached him. "Yes, I am. What's your name, miss?"

She grasped his outstretched hand, her smile brightening. "I'm Chelsea. Oh my God. My friends and I come to your shows almost every week. They are never going to believe I met you!"

"That's always good to hear. Thanks for supporting us." He offered the young waitress a friendly smile, even as he felt the coolness rolling off Lina's body like an incoming snowstorm.

A squeal of delight escaped Chelsea's mouth. She reached into her apron pocket and pulled out a small notebook with a floral patterned cover. Opening the pad, she held it out along with her pen. "Would you please sign this for me?"

He hazarded a quick glance at Lina, who was making a show of reading her magazine with rapt interest. Her irritation was easy to detect from the tightness of her face and the way her eyes darted rapidly across the pages. Resisting the urge to chuckle, he took the items from Chelsea and signed her book as she'd asked.

As he handed the book back to her, she hugged it against her chest for a moment, her broad smile a testament to her level of excitement. After taking a few deep breaths, she switched back to her order pad. "What can I get for you?"

"I'll have the vegetarian manicotti lunch special and a mineral water, please."

"No problem. It'll be right out." Chelsea, having jotted his order down, turned and moved toward the kitchen.

After the waitress's departure, he turned his gaze back on his sullen date, who was still pretending to pore over her open magazine. "Lina."

She looked up when he called her name. "Yes?"

"Is there a problem?"

She pursed her lips for a moment, and then stated simply, "No."

His eyebrow hitched. Did she really think he hadn't noticed her frosty demeanor toward the waitress? He folded his arms over his chest, watching her, and waited.

A few silent moments later, she took the bait. "What? Why are you looking at me like that?"

"I couldn't help noticing how your attitude changed once the waitress started talking about being a fan of the band."

Her tawny eyes widened, then rolled dramatically. "I didn't say anything to her, Rashad."

"I know. But you didn't look particularly happy about it, either."

"I didn't realize I was supposed to jump for joy

whenever one of your little groupies starts fangirling over you."

He groaned. "Lina—"

She put up her open palm, signaling that she didn't want to hear any more. "Look, I'd really like to finish this article I'm reading, if you don't mind. You can lecture me later."

He shook his head. She had to be the most stubborn, headstrong woman he'd ever had the pleasure of tangling with, and he wouldn't change that for the world. "Fine, I'll keep quiet—for now."

She cut him a censuring look, then let her gaze drop back to the magazine.

Chelsea returned with their drinks, but didn't linger. Rashad figured she sensed the tension at the table. He was scrolling through his phone while his tight-lipped companion read from her magazine.

Just about the time he began to worry that Lina could hear his stomach's growling demands for food, Chelsea approached the table with their two steaming plates. When she'd set the food before them and made sure they didn't need anything else, she made herself scarce.

At this point he was too famished to argue with Lina, but as he dug into his manicotti, he vowed to set her straight once his hunger was allayed. They ate in relative silence, except for a few comments about how good the food tasted.

Once they'd finished, he paid their check and stood from his seat. Rounding the table to where she sat, he pulled out her chair. She got up, gathered her purse, her phone and the magazine, and the two of them left the restaurant.

Outside on the sidewalk, they walked side by side. A good number of people were out walking their dogs, going in and out of shops, or returning to work from their lunch breaks. Clouds were beginning to gather, signaling one of the pop-up afternoon thunderstorms so common during a North Carolina summer. The softly blowing breeze carried the scent of incoming rain.

He reached for her hand, but the rolled up magazine she clutched stopped him from grasping it. Having had enough of her funky attitude, he stopped midstep. Placing a gentle hold on her arm, he moved them both to the right to get out of the way of the other foot traffic. There, under the red-and-white-striped awning that sheltered the entrance of a candy shop, he used his fingertips to tilt her chin so he could look into her eyes.

"Baby, what is bothering you?"

The remnants of a frown remained on her face. "Rashad, not now."

"Yes, now."

"But—"

He smothered her protests by placing his lips to hers. Her soft mouth yielded to his, and he tasted a hint of fruity sweetness there—a combination of the lemonade she'd been drinking and the berry flavored gloss on her lips. He lingered there, his tongue plumbing the depths of her mouth until she gave a muffled moan. Only then did he release her.

Her cheeks were tinted with red, and she seemed flustered. "You can't just kiss me like that in public."

"Why not?"

In response, her cheeks reddened even more.

"Well, I've got bad news for you, baby. Either tell me what's wrong, or I'm going to keep kissing you just like that, for everyone to see."

She blinked several times. "You'd make me late for work."

"Damn straight."

Her head dropped back with a dramatic sigh. "Fine. I'm not so thrilled about the groupies, I never was. I get that it comes with the territory of being in a band, but that doesn't mean I have to like it."

He placed his open palms on her shoulders, running his hands up and down the length of her bare arms. "Lina. No matter how many women come up to me, you're the only one I want."

Her eyes softened. "So you say."

"So I mean. You've got to trust me, baby. It's the only way this thing between us is going to work out."

She tilted her head to the side, a small smile lifting the corners of her mouth. "Make me believe you."

So he gathered her into his arms, and beneath the shadow of the awning, kissed her with all the passion he had inside.

## Chapter 7

Back at the law office, Lina knew she was dangerously close to being late for what her boss had described as a very important office meeting. Taking in her reflection in the ladies' room mirror, she sighed at her disheveled state. The impromptu post-lunch make out session with Rashad had not only left her breathless, she now resembled a teenager sneaking in after a late-night tryst. Shaking her head, she set out to fix what Rashad had messed up.

While she worked on getting herself together, her mind replayed those torrid moments under the candy store awning. She recalled the softness of his lips, the sensual stroking of his tongue inside her mouth, the arousing way he'd cupped her hip with his big hand. His skillful, possessive kisses had almost made her forget that they were kissing on the streets of downtown Charlotte in broad daylight. She chuckled to herself.

*He sure knows how to get his point across.*

After she'd corrected her smudged lip gloss, runny mascara and mussed hair, she popped a mint into her mouth. Then she slung the strap of her handbag over her shoulder and walked out into the corridor.

She entered the boardroom a few moments later. She greeted her colleagues, most of whom were already present, and took her usual seat on the right side of the rectangular table, toward the center. Lerner was one of the smaller firms in the area, with a total of twenty-one people on staff, and Lina had been at the firm long enough to have established a professional relationship with most of them. She didn't know the five members of the secretarial staff all that well, but that was due to high turnover in their department.

At present, only two seats remained empty now, the one across from her belonging to Tara Mitchell, and the one at the head of the table where Mrs. Lerner sat. Lina had just enough time to settle into her seat, open her briefcase and take out a legal pad and pen before the two missing associates entered the room and took their respective seats.

Mrs. Lerner called the meeting to order, then passed the reigns over to her administrative assistant to go over the case files from the previous week. Lina listened intently, making a note of each case number, the attorney who'd handled it, and the outcome, even though she knew a dossier of this information would be distributed at the end of the month. Keeping good notes was simply her way of keeping her mind sharp during each meeting which, at times, were incredibly boring. She continued taking notes through most of the meeting, filling five of the sheets on her lavender-tinted legal pad. The sound of Mrs. Lerner clearing her throat made her set the pen aside and look up.

"Now let's move on to some exciting news. I want to congratulate the two junior partners who are being promoted to senior partners, effective in two weeks."

Lina looked around the room.

She didn't have to wait long before Mrs. Lerner spoke again.

"Some say I rarely smile, but I'm very proud of the efforts of these two women, who are assets to our firm. Please join me in applauding Lina Smith-Todd and Tara Mitchell."

Lina stood and looked across the table to the beaming Tara, who also stood. As their coworkers feted them with clapping and cheers, Lina felt the pride swelling in her chest. This was the moment she'd been waiting for. The moment when the all-nighters she'd pulled in undergrad and in law school, the long hours poring over law texts and depositions, and the social life she'd all but abandoned finally paid off.

Yes, this was a game changer. Making senior partner in a respected law firm as a black woman under forty was no small feat, and she planned to celebrate this accomplishment to the fullest. Part of that celebration would be to purchase Thelonious Monk's baby grand, and revel in the look of utter joy the piano would surely put on her mother's face.

The applause tapered off as Mrs. Lerner gestured for everyone's attention. "That's it for today, people. Let's get back to work. We'll celebrate with a little cake at lunch time."

As the group began to disperse, Lina took a moment to walk over to Tara and shake her hand. "Congratulations, Tara."

Tara, a forty-something mother of two grown sons, smiled in response. "Thanks, Lina. Congratulations to you, as well."

They chatted for a few moments while Tara gathered her things, and then the two of them strolled toward the door.

Mrs. Lerner stopped Lina.

With a wave, Tara disappeared from the room.

The lead attorney addressed her. "Lina, I want to talk to you a moment. I'm having my assistant place the order today for updated signage and stationery for the firm. What's the situation with your name?"

She didn't hesitate. "I'm coming in late tomorrow morning because I'm going to the courthouse first thing to drop my ex-husband's name." Sure, Warren had helped finance her first year of law school, but that didn't negate his numerous infidelities. She was stepping into a new season of her life, and she refused to do so while still carrying the burden of his last name.

"Very good. I don't want to hold up the printing process, so I'll tell my assistant to have everything printed up with 'Lerner, Mitchell and Smith.' Just be sure to bring me a copy of your name-change paperwork when you come in tomorrow."

"No problem." Lina shook hands with her boss and exited the boardroom.

As she walked down the corridor toward her office, her phone chimed, signaling an incoming text message. She grabbed the knob on her office door and twisted, pushing it open. Inside, she moved over to the desk, set her purse down on top, and fished the phone out of it. She unlocked the touch screen. A smile touched her lips when she saw the message was from Rashad.

I'm having a HARD time concentrating this afternoon.

Her smile widened as she typed her reply.

You're the one who decided to make your point with kisses.

She set the phone down on the edge of the desk, but before she could walk away it chimed again with his reply.

You know you liked it, baby.

Shaking her head, she sent him back a winky face emoji and tucked her phone away. If they kept this up, neither of them would get any work done. She hoped he'd go back to whatever he'd been doing, to keep her whole afternoon from being mired in distraction.

He didn't text her again, but the memory of his soft lips and the feeling of his hands on her body still lingered in her mind for the rest of the afternoon.

\* \* \*

As the end of the workday drew near on Wednesday, Rashad found himself wringing his hands. It wasn't something he did often, but his nerves were frazzled, and for good reason. In less than fifteen minutes, there would be an end-of-day departmental meeting for the register of deeds office. And he knew that during that meeting, he'd have to do the very thing he'd been dreading since this most recent round of budget cuts had been announced: tell someone they were out of a job.

Draining the cup of cold water he'd gotten from the cooler, he sighed. He'd been raised with a very strong work ethic, as well as a sense of responsibility to give to others. Still, there were not many people in the world who demonstrated the high level of commitment, self-sacrifice, and professionalism that his family demanded from him. Rick Havens was one of those rare people, and the prospect of having to tell the older man he'd be losing his job in two weeks made Rashad feel like shit.

He stood from his seat behind the desk, straightened his tie and left his office. As he strode down the corridor toward the conference room, he truly wished Gary were there to do this decidedly dirty work. His boss had left earlier to accompany his mother-in-law to a follow-up appointment. Being the most senior employee present that afternoon meant he'd drawn the short straw.

Inside the conference room, most of the staff was already seated around the long rectangular table. As

Rashad took his seat at the head, he took in the faces of his colleagues. They were all good people, and most were hard workers. Sure, Claudia was the office gossip who always had her ears open to everyone's conversations, and Maynard—who hadn't yet arrived—was habitually five or ten minutes late to everything. But those things were pretty minor. As a supervisor, Rashad wasn't one to demand perfection from his staff. All he wanted was for them to do their jobs to the best of their abilities and nine and a half times out of ten, they delivered.

By the time five o'clock rolled around everyone was present. Rashad then stood and cleared his throat. "I'm going to be brief, since I know we'd all like to get home. Gary has informed me that the county is ready to begin the first round of staff cuts. It's not just us, this same speech is being given in several other departments in the courthouse today."

A collective groan rose from the people sitting around the table.

Rashad nodded. "I know, I'm not happy about this, either. But as I'm told we have no choice. For right now, our office only has to cut two positions, and fortunately we're able to give two weeks' notice and one month's severance pay."

For the rest of the meeting, Rashad outlined some of the changes that would take place around the office. Budget-cutting measures were being put in place, such as transitioning to a mostly paperless office, and cutting back on overtime.

Rashad leaned his back against the whitewashed

wall and took a few questions from his employees. Most wanted to know if and when more cuts would be made. Unfortunately, that wasn't something he had a ready answer for. Information was being funneled to him through Gary, who was getting it from the suits at county in snatches.

After the meeting was adjourned, he asked two of his employees to stay behind.

Rick Havens stood from his seat, making eye contact with him. "Let me guess. You're about to tell me I'm officially retired."

Even as he wished things could be different, Rashad offered a solemn nod. "I'm sorry, Rick. But I still have two weeks to figure something out for you, and I plan to keep my promise."

Rick responded with a solemn nod. "Let me know what you come up with, Mac."

Rashad's eyes fell on Nathan, the office's young courier. "Sorry, Nate. We're going to have to cut your position as well."

The cocky young brother responded with a chuckle. "It's all good, boss man. I'm about to get my degree in December, so I'll be all right."

"I respect your positive outlook, Nate."

Within the next half hour, Rashad locked the door to the empty conference room and returned to his office. As was often the case, he was the last person remaining in the office. It was just after 6 p.m., and he didn't want to linger any longer. Once he'd gathered his belongings, he left, locking the main office door behind him.

In the parking deck, he retrieved his truck and got on the road toward home. The meeting had left a sense of sadness hanging over him like a dark cloud. He could still see the look of disappointment on Rick Havens's face. What was the world coming to when even an excellent employee like Rick had no job security?

To break up the burden of gloom sitting on his shoulder, he used the Bluetooth in his truck to call Lina. He didn't know if she was still at work this late, but he felt a strange, yet compelling need to hear her voice.

"Hello?"

The moment her sultry voice filled the cabin of his truck, he felt some of the tightness in his upper body melt away. "Hi, baby. I hope you're not busy."

"I'm home. I'm just about to throw on a stir-fry for dinner. What's up?"

"I just wanted to hear your voice."

There was a moment of silence on the line, except for the sounds of her banging around in her kitchen. "Really?"

"Yes. It was a rough day at the office. I had to fire one of our oldest and best employees due to these asinine budget cuts."

"Oh, no. I'm sorry, Rashad."

The sympathy in her tone went a long way toward soothing his frustrations. "I appreciate that."

"Hmm." The sound she made came over the speakers, making him think she was contemplating something.

"What is it?"

"Isn't there anything you can do for the man? Maybe

there's still a way you can save his job and keep your office on budget."

He spun the steering wheel as he made the right turn into his neighborhood. Her words got him thinking, and there was only one solution he could come up with. Remembering his promise to Rick, he made up his mind. "You're right, Lina. I think there is something I can do."

She responded with an upbeat tone. "Great. Let me know how it turns out."

What he planned to do for Rick had a very high probability of saving the older man's job; still, he had no idea how people would react to his actions. Regardless of that unknown, he would do it anyway. As a man of his word and as a grateful employer, he owed it to Rick.

"Why don't you come by the Blue Lounge for the Gents show Friday night? It's been a while since you've heard us play."

"I do love live jazz. Sure, I'll swing by."

"Great. Then I'll see you there, baby. Thanks for listening."

She chuckled. "You're welcome."

He disconnected the call, and his satellite radio began to play again. Oddly enough, Monk's original version of "'Round Midnight" vibrated through his car speakers on the all-jazz station the radio was set to.

Hearing Monk's signature composition brought back thoughts of the priceless baby grand locked up in Cleveland and Wendell. There were now only a few days left until the rescheduled auction would take place. Honestly, Lina's glossy lips and dangerous curves had occupied his thoughts so much lately that he hadn't spent that much time plotting to get his hands on the piano. The song served as a reminder of all the things he'd need to set into motion to make sure he'd win the bidding.

He wanted that piano, but she seemed to want it just as badly, and he had a feeling that no matter who won the bidding, there would likely be some degree of drama between them. That was why he'd invited her to the Gents show—he'd spend that evening wooing her in hopes of cutting down on hard feelings once he took home the prized piano.

He hummed along to the song as he pulled into his garage. After he cut the engine and made sure the garage door was closed, he entered the house through the side door.

The next several days were bound to be interesting.

# Chapter 8

As Lina entered Bar 10 Thursday evening for the monthly meeting of her book club, she saw most of the members were already present. Eve, Ophelia and Denise were all lounging in the overstuffed cream-colored armchairs in the back corner of the space. Every month they sat in those same seats, away from the entrance and the main common area of the establishment. The chairs were arranged in a semicircle around a short-legged coffee table, allowing the ladies optimum positioning for their lively conversations.

Lina crossed the room and slipped into an empty seat, setting her camel leather tote on the floor next to the chair. "Hey, girls."

The women exchanged greetings and pleasantries for a few moments, catching up with each other on the happenings of the past four weeks. Lina fetched a glass and served herself from the open bottle of Mondavi Cabernet Sauvignon on the table. Large bowls of popcorn, pretzels and sweet and salty trail mix accompanied the wine, as was the usual fare for their meetings.

"Eve, you're still glowing with happiness, girl." Ophelia sipped from her wineglass as she made the observation.

In response, Eve's already wide grin brightened even more. "We had such a wonderful time in the islands. This private beach, the personal butler and that cozy little villa right on the water..." Her voice trailed off as her eyes took on a dreamy, faraway look.

Lina couldn't help smiling. She and Eve had been best friends for years, and she was genuinely happy for her. This was the first time she'd seen Eve since she returned from her seven-week island honeymoon, and she knew there would be more steamy details to come. Lina wondered if she'd ever get to that place of bliss with Rashad. She didn't realize she'd sighed out loud until Denise called her on it.

Between bites of popcorn, Denise asked, "Lina, what's up with you, girl?"

Three sets of curious eyes landed squarely on Lina's face.

She closed her eyes briefly to prepare for the onslaught of questions she knew were coming.

Then she got a brief reprieve, in the form of the last member's arrival.

"Sorry I'm late, girls." Fiona dropped her small

clutch on the coffee table and eased down into the last empty armchair. "What'd I miss?"

Ophelia smirked. "A little taste of Eve's honeymoon, but you're just in time to hear all about what's going on with Lina and Rashad."

Fiona's hazel eyes widened then swung to Lina. "Girl! You and Rashad are back together?"

Lina nodded, chuckling. "Sorry I didn't tell you, but I know how busy you are with grad school. Plus I just assumed the Mouth of the South over there would tell you." She gestured to Denise, who had the decency to look sheepish.

Eve waved a French manicured hand dismissively. "Yeah, yeah. We all know you're back together. Now tell us what's happening!"

Crossing her legs and settling back into her chair, Lina began. "We've only been back together for a hot minute, it hasn't even been two whole weeks. So far, everything is going pretty well."

"How did y'all end up getting back together, anyway?" Denise said as she munched on popcorn and leaned forward in her chair as if she were watching a movie.

The question made Lina think about the object that had brought them together in the first place: Monk's piano. "We both showed up at an auction to bid on a piano once owned by Thelonious Monk. The bidding was interrupted, and I guess one thing led to another."

"What happened with the piano?" Eve asked.

"The auction house has been shut down, since the

owner and the auctioneer were injured in a car wreck. Right now, no one has purchased it."

"Enough about the piano." Fiona chuckled. "Come on now, Lina. You know we want details. Have you given up the cookie yet?"

Draining her wineglass, Eve hit Fiona with a mean side-eye. "Girl, that's just uncouth."

"Whatever. Just spill the beans," Denise encouraged.

Lina shook her head. "No, I haven't slept with him yet. This thing is still pretty new."

"No, it isn't. You got with him when you dated before, and as I recall, he could swing the D with the best of them." Eve winked.

With a dramatic roll of her eyes, Lina groaned. "Can y'all find your way out of my business so we can discuss the book? We are a book club, right?"

Denise nodded in agreement. "As president I must agree with Lina. Let's get to the book discussion. How many of you finished it?" She reached into her bag and held up her copy of Brenda Jackson's latest novel.

Lina raised her hand, and noted that everyone else had finished the book with the exception of Eve.

Wearing the soft smile of a satisfied woman, Eve admitted, "I'm only halfway through it. Darius has been keeping me very…busy."

The group of women exchanged knowing glances.

As the conversation finally turned to the book, Lina felt a modicum of relief. She loved the girls in her book club, even though they were nosy as hell. Things were going well with Rashad, but as she'd said, it was all very new. She wasn't really in the mood or position to have long discussions with her girls about him, since she wasn't quite sure where things were heading this time around.

There was one thing she was sure of. Rashad was about as sexy as a man could be, and it had been a long time since she'd been properly pleasured. Every time he crossed her mind, she remembered what it had been like to be with him, all those months ago when they'd first attempted a relationship. Despite all the time that had passed, she could still easily recall his prowess in the bedroom. He was the knight and she was the dragon, he slayed her. Every. Single. Time.

She remembered the first time they'd made love. He'd fixed her a romantic candlelight dinner on fine china at his house. After they'd eaten, he'd taken her out on the balcony. The moon that night had been full, the sky filled with stars sparkling like diamonds. It wasn't long before he'd skillfully coaxed her dress up around her waist. She could still feel his hands, his lips. He'd taken his time getting her ready. Only after she'd succumbed to orgasm did he give her what she had been begging for. He'd made slow, sweet love to her while she was draped over his balcony railing…

"Lina. Lina!"

The sound of Fiona snapping her fingers jerked Lina out of her fantasy world and back to reality.

Fiona quipped, "Fantasize much?"

Lina rolled her eyes. "Hush. Stop teasing me. What did you say?"

Eve giggled. "She asked you what you thought of the sex…"

"Dang it, y'all—"

"…in the book. She was talking about the sex in the book, girl." At this point, Eve could barely keep a straight face.

Swallowing hard, Lina dropped her head. She had been thinking about sex, but it certainly wasn't the sex in the book, and everybody knew it. Not knowing what else to say, she fell back on the line often used by her clients when they were approached by the press. "No comment."

The rest of the girls erupted into peals of laughter.

Drawing back the heavy blue velvet curtain just a bit, Rashad peeked out of the small opening. The house lights in the Blue Lounge were still up as people arrived for the night's performance. From the looks of it, the Gents would be playing to another sold-out house. Ticket sales were usually very high on Friday nights, and tonight was no exception. He let his eyes scan the crowd, looking for Lina.

It wasn't long before he spotted her. She was seated near the front, just left of center stage. Her chair was turned sideways from the table, toward the stage, and as he took in the sight of her, he felt his body temperature rising. She had her curls pinned up, and wore a sexy little black tube dress. The cut of the dress revealed the curve of her shoulders, the tempting tops of her breasts, and the long honey-brown legs he'd love to have wrapped around his waist. On her feet were a pair of black stilettos that revealed just the tips of her shimmery red toenails.

He swallowed hard, knowing he should be setting up his keyboard and mic stand. He could stare at her fine ass all night long. She looked gorgeous, and he just hoped he could get through the show without pouncing on her like a hungry tiger.

A firm tap on his shoulder jarred him out of his erotic fantasies. He turned his head and saw Ken, the drummer, staring at him.

"Dude, what are you doing? Get your shit together for the show." Ken's expression belied his amusement.

"Sorry, I'm coming."

Ken slid past him and got a look at the crowd. "Oh, I see your problem. Lina's out there, and dressed to kill." He paused, made a whistling sound. "Try to get it together, man."

Rashad threw a fake punch at his friend to reward him for his chiding. "Scram, Ken."

As Ken walked away, Rashad released the curtain and let it fall back into place again. He really did need to get ready at this point. He made his way to center stage, and spent a few minutes setting up his keyboard and the mic stand. Then adjusted everything to its proper positioning. Around him, his bandmates did the same. Ken adjusted the various components of his drum set. Darius set up the support stand for his upright bass. Marco looped the strap of his saxophone around his neck and played a few notes, tuning the instrument.

After setting the tall stool he used during shows

behind the keyboard, Rashad drew a deep breath. He and his bandmates had been at this so long, he was well past preshow jitters. Still, knowing Lina was sitting right in the front row had him feeling a whole new kind of trepidation. Just like the first night she'd come to the Blue all those months ago, he wanted to impress her. Now the stakes were even higher. She was giving their relationship a second chance, and the last thing he wanted to do was blow it.

She'd made it clear that she didn't care for the band's female fans, who were often stuck to him because he was the main vocalist. She'd called them "groupies," as he recalled. That word had some pretty negative connotations, and he preferred to just call them fans. After all, the Gents weren't some band of teenage rockers, trawling the concert circuit for booze and loose women. They were a jazz quartet, and they were all much too mature for those kinds of shenanigans.

He straightened his bright red tie and adjusted his fedora. He could hear the night's emcee introducing them, and he glanced around to his three friends. They were all poised in position as he was, knowing the curtain would rise at any second.

As the blue velvet curtain ascended, revealing the band to the waiting audience, Rashad stepped into the red-tinged spotlight, the mic in his hand. "Evening, ladies and gentlemen. Let's get this thing started, shall we?"

Boisterous applause met his greeting, and as the sound died down, he fixed his eyes on Lina. He could only see an outline of her, due to the stage lights, but that was inspiration enough. He kept his eyes on her as he plied the keys of his keyboard, playing the opening notes of the night's first song, George and Ira Gershwin's "Embraceable You." The band joined in, one instrument at a time, until they all were playing. Opening his mouth, he tilted his head back and belted the verse.

The lighting made it impossible to make out her facial expression, but he could see her swaying to the music. That was good enough for him, and he gave the performance his all. The song ended to thunderous applause, and more than a few appreciative female shouts.

As the show went on, moving into a few instrumental numbers so Rashad could rest his voice, a number of female fans left their seats to lean over the front edge of the stage. The Blue was an intimate venue, meaning that only mere inches separated his wing tips from the extended hands of some of the women. He eased back a bit, hoping to avoid stepping on anyone's fingers, while offering the ladies a convivial smile.

When he swung his eyes in Lina's direction again, he noticed that she'd stopped swaying, and was now perched stiffly in her chair. Something told him that the change in her demeanor might be due to the swarm of fans at his feet. But at the moment, there wasn't much he could do about it. He decided that if Lina was indeed perturbed by the fans' behavior, he would give her something that would assure her, once and for all, that he only had eyes for her.

The set finally drew to a close, and Rashad caught a last glimpse of a sullen-looking Lina as the house lights were turned on and the curtain dropped. Determined that he would settle this "groupie" thing with her, he packed up his instrument and equipment at lightning speed.

He was on his way through the backstage area toward the lounge when Darius called after him.

"Wanna go to the Bull with us for drinks?"

Rashad didn't stop walking and barely turned his head as he called back, "Rain check."

With the large case holding his keyboard and stand in one hand, he pushed through the door into the main area of the lounge, just in time to catch a glimpse of Lina's back as she headed out the side door. He picked up his pace, taking long strides until he caught up with her just outside the club.

"Lina." He placed a gentle hand on her arm.

She turned her honey-gold eyes on him, and he could see she was upset. "What is it, Rashad?"

"Where are you rushing off to?"

"Home. I don't really have any desire to see you flirting with the groupies tonight."

He sighed, set the heavy case down by his feet. "Baby, we talked about this. They're not groupies. Who do you think I am, some swell-headed youngin' out here chasing tail?"

She frowned, folding her arms across her chest. "No, but you don't have to look like you're enjoying the attention so much."

He pressed a hand to his temple. "Really? Would you rather I scowl at them, Lina?"

She turned her head, looking away from him, but said nothing.

He placed his hands on either side of her waist and pulled her rigid body close to his. "I don't want any of them, baby. You're the only one I want. And if you don't believe me, then let me show you."

Her stiff body softened within his embrace, as did the hardness in her eyes. She tilted her head, looked up at him. "And how do you plan to do that?"

He leaned down, bringing his lips close to her ear. Softly, he declared, "By making love to you so thoroughly, you'll never doubt me again."

A visible shiver shot through her body.

A moment later, when his lips touched hers, she put up no protest. He held her close, and she wound her graceful arms around his neck. He kissed her with all the passion he held inside, his tongue sweeping through the sweet cavern of her mouth. She'd been drinking champagne during the show, and he tasted the lingering tartness of it as he devoured her mouth.

When he finally pulled away, a few silent beats passed as they simply stood near the building, gazing into each other's eyes.

Finally, she spoke. "I went back to my maiden name a couple of days ago."

"I'm glad to hear it." Though he didn't know why she was telling him that now, he was pleased to know she'd severed that tie to her past. "So what do you want to do now?"

"Follow me to my house." As the words left her glossy lips, her fingertips lightly played through his dreadlocks. Then her hand dropped away, and she fixed him with a come-hither stare so potent, his groin tightened.

Not needing to be asked twice, Rashad got his case and strode to his car.

## Chapter 9

Lina couldn't remember the last time she'd driven so fast, but as she twisted her key in the lock of her front door, she didn't have a care. Rashad must have been going just as fast to keep up with her.

The solid mass of Rashad's body, pressed against her back, removed all interest in regret, or in anything that wasn't related to getting him naked as soon as possible.

Once the door was shut and relocked behind them, she only had a moment to get her breath before he swept her into his strong arms. His lips crashed down on hers with such intensity, only his embrace kept her from swooning and hitting the floor. One of his large hands wove its way into her curls, massaging her scalp, while the other firmly gripped her behind. Both touches were possessive, insistent and oh so sexy.

He separated the seal of their lips, backing her up against the wall of her entryway alcove. The space was occupied by nothing more than a painting on the wall and a small console table. As he swept her dish of potpourri on the floor and set her down, she discovered the table was just wide enough to accommodate her hips. Once she was seated, he moved in, his soft lips trailing hot kisses over her neck, shoulder and collarbone. When he tugged down the top of her dress to reveal her breasts, she gasped. But as his warm mouth captured one of her nipples, she could do nothing but moan while he melted her insides. Liquid warmth pooled between her legs, dampening the lacy swath of her panties.

Once he'd given the same devoted attention to her other breast, he drew back for a moment. Through hooded eyes, she watched him take off his fedora and sport coat, hanging them on the antique coatrack she kept by her front door. Loosening and removing his tie, he then stripped away his button-down shirt and the tank beneath, revealing the rippled musculature of his chest and abdomen.

Her eyes traveled to his low-slung trousers. They sat on his waist in such a way that she could see the cuts in the muscle where his thighs met his pelvis, and as far as she could tell, he wasn't wearing any underwear. She sucked in a breath as she saw the bulge of his hardness, imprinted against the dark fabric.

Clad in only the trousers, wing tips and socks, he eased back toward her, dropping to his knees on the carpeted floor.

She'd been down this road with him before, and

when she realized what he was about to do, her whole body began to shake of its own accord. He inched closer and closer, until his chest touched her knees.

"Open up for me, baby. Let me show you how I really feel." He placed an open palm on each trembling knee, but didn't press her.

Her legs parted on their own, as her hips lifted from the polished surface of the table. He reached up to raise her dress. Then he proceeded to tug her cream-colored lace panties away from her body, tossing them aside.

In the dim light cast by her entryway lamp, she could see his glittering eyes, and the smile touching the corners of his soft lips. His right hand left her hip, and before she could brace herself, his fingertips were playing through the damp vent between her thighs. Soft moans escaped her throat at his skillful touch. She had not been with a man since she and Rashad had broken up, and now she knew why. There was no other man on this earth who could touch her this way. And she knew from experience that this was just a warm-up for him.

Her head dropped back as the magic of his touch overtook her. He slipped two of his long fingers inside her, and she nearly buckled at the charge of pleasure that ran through her.

His deep, rumbling chuckle rose in the silence as he withdrew. "Don't worry, baby. I won't make you suffer for long."

He leaned forward and let the tip of his tongue sweep through her damp folds.

The initial contact tore a long, shaky moan from her lips.

His big hands lifted her thighs up onto his shoulders, then gripped her ass to stabilize her. While he worked his mouth on her, it was all she could do not to slide down the wall and onto the floor in a heap. Her back arched like a bow, and she laced her fingers into the dark length of his dreadlocks.

It wasn't long until orgasm shot through her. The whole world rocked, her hips rose from the tabletop as she screamed his name into the silence of the house.

She was boneless and witless, but aware of him lifting her up and carrying her across the room. As her naked hips came to rest on the overstuffed sofa, she opened her eyes. She watched with rapt desire as he kicked off his wing tips, then rid himself of his socks. As he loosened his belt and tugged his slacks down, she saw that he was wearing underwear—low-cut black bikinis that barely contained his raging hardness. She swallowed as he snatched off the underwear, letting his manhood spring free. It was as long, thick and beautiful as she remembered, and just as hard and ready for her as it had been when he had visited her dreams.

She watched him remove a condom packet from the pocket of his discarded pants, then open it. He unrolled it, covering himself, without ever taking his eyes off her face.

She felt her tongue dart out to dampen her lips. *This man is so fine.*

He reached for her, turned her around. "Now, as I recall, this is how my baby likes to be loved."

He was right, and she couldn't be gladder that he'd remembered. She sighed with anticipation as she let him position her on her knees with her back to him. She draped her upper body over the back cushions of her sofa, feeling the seat beneath her give as he knelt behind her. He used his fingertips to open her once again, then slipped inside her in one long, smooth stroke.

Having him inside her again was like the most welcome of homecomings. Her body bloomed to him, drawing him deeper, where she most wanted him to be. He groaned as her muscles clamped down on him. Soft sighs of ecstasy escaped her throat with every thrust of his powerful hips.

She gripped the back of the sofa as his arms held fast to her waist. The loving he gave her now surpassed even the most erotic memories she'd had from their past together. He had her shaking, moaning, calling out his name. It was as if he were on a mission to make her lose her mind. If that were his goal, she'd fall happily into the pit of insanity. Do whatever he wanted, so the loving wouldn't stop.

He splayed a hand through her hair, drew her head back to whisper in her ear.

"Only you, baby."

His declaration, delivered in that sex-drenched baritone, pushed her over the edge. She cried out as another orgasm grabbed hold of her and tossed her up into the stratosphere.

In the aftermath, she simply lay against the cushions, trying to get her breath. His hard body remained against her back. At first the only sounds were of their shaky breaths.

Then he asked, "Do you believe me yet?"

She swallowed, exhaled. Her mouth wanted to speak but her mind had been reduced to mush.

"Then let's go to the bedroom and 'discuss' this further." He eased away from her.

When she turned his way, she saw him standing there naked in front of her sofa, his hand outstretched. Reaching out, she took it and let him lead her into her bedroom.

Rashad took in the familiar sights and smells of Lina's bedroom as he stepped inside, still holding her hand. He hadn't been in this room in a long while, and he was glad she'd allowed him to reenter her world. Taking a seat on the edge of the bed, he gestured for her to sit next to him.

She obliged, looking at him with wide eyes. "I don't know if I can take much more of your convincing, Rashad."

He chuckled. Already his manhood was thickening just from being so close to her nude beauty. "When I asked if you believed me, you hesitated."

She shook her head. "No, I didn't. I just couldn't speak."

His eyebrow cocked. "Oh, really?"

Her cheeks reddened, and she looked away, her long fringe of dark lashes lowering. "Stop teasing me."

He draped his arm around her shoulders. "It's like I told you, Lina. I don't want anyone else but you. And if you still have doubts, I have all night to show you just how serious I am."

And he meant it. Making love to her was a privilege,

and one he was more than happy to exercise again, and all through the night. He loved the way she moaned, the way she sighed, the way her body rose to his touch.

*Damn. I love her.*

He'd always been a flirt, always enjoyed the chase when it came to women. But when it came to her, things were different. He encircled her with his arms, leaned down to place kisses on the soft, fragrant skin of her neck and shoulders, inhaling her scent all the while. The musical sounds of her sighs filled the room, and his manhood stiffened even more.

She pulled away, sucked on her bottom lip. Her eyes held heat and desire. "Maybe I could use just a little more assurance."

He watched, enraptured, as she stood before him. She opened her palm and placed it flat against the center of his chest, applying the slightest pressure.

Taking the hint, he lay on his back across the bed.

From her bedside table, she produced a fresh condom. Doing away with the old one, she slowly rolled the new one down over his engorged manhood. Watching her cover him was an extremely erotic sight, one that made anticipation crackle through him.

By the time she climbed atop him and sank down onto him, he had to restrain himself to keep the act from being over before it got started. The heated tightness of her body engulfed him, and he filled his hands with the fullness of her hips as she started to ride.

He forced his hooded eyes to remain open, so he could watch the rise and fall of her beautiful body. She was a glorious sight. Her head tossed back, breasts bouncing, and her arms stretched above her head as she gave herself over to pleasure. The song of her moans rang sweet in his ears, mingled with his own groans.

The sounds she made became longer, more intense and louder, until finally, her orgasm came with a sensual cry. The contractions of her inner muscles sent him into spasms of his own, and he gripped her hips and closed his eyes as his body splintered with release.

She lay down atop him, her breasts pressed against his chest, and he wrapped his arms around her. Holding her close to his rapidly beating heart felt right, natural. She made him feel complete, made him feel like he could do anything. What more could he ask for in a woman?

Her soft snores let him know she had fallen asleep, so he remained where he was to avoid disturbing her. While asleep, she looked as innocent as a newborn. He knew better, though. She was as fiery and passionate a woman as he'd ever met. He felt he knew her well, probably better than some of her friends did.

But she did not know all there was to know about him. Perceptive as she was, she knew he'd been keeping something from her back when they first attempted a relationship. He had been dishonest with her, but not about seeing other women as she'd thought. No, his secret was much more complex than that, and he had no idea how she would react when she finally discovered it. Because of that, he planned to sit on his truth for as long as possible.

She stirred a bit, and he held her a little tighter. Looking at her, naked and sated from his loving, he knew he could never be unfaithful to her. What they shared was rare, special. He would never dishonor that by being with other women. He just hoped that to-night's "convincing" had been sufficient means to show her that he was ready to commit to her, fully.

"Wow." She uttered the single word in a sleep-filled voice.

A smile spread across his face. "So you liked that, huh?"

The sound she made in response was like the sound someone made when they sank their teeth into their very favorite dessert—the sound of utter and complete satisfaction.

"Glad to hear it." He loved hearing her make that sound, loved knowing he'd shown her the heights of passion. If she'd let him, he'd be willing to spend the rest of his life gifting her with that pleasure, every single night.

Those thoughts of forever gave him pause. He'd been ready to commit to her the first time they'd been in a relationship, yet she couldn't see it. She let her mistrust come between them, and as much as he cared about her, he had no guarantee that wouldn't happen again.

Loving her and losing her once had hurt. If he had to go through that again, it would surely kill him. This time around, he planned to guard his feelings as best he could, because he didn't plan to go out like that again.

## Chapter 10

Taking a sip of her coffee, Lina flipped over the contract page she'd been poring over and moved on to the next. She gave the page her complete focus as she read through the clauses, separated by sections and bullet points. A client of hers had requested that she perform one last contract evaluation before the document was finalized. It wasn't the most enjoyable task, but it was a vital part of the practice of employment law. Mondays always seemed to bring a bumper crop of new contracts and paperwork to be handled.

She was so engrossed in the paperwork that she didn't immediately hear the rapping on her office door. When she noticed it, she looked up. "Come in."

Mrs. Lerner walked in, holding a large cardboard

box. "Good news, Lina. The new stationery finally came in. Want to see it?"

Setting the contract aside, Lina stood. "Of course!" She got a pair of scissors from her desk caddy and cut through the packing tape.

Mrs. Lerner flung the flaps open and pulled out several smaller boxes inside the large one. There were business cards, ink pens, folders and more. All were emblazoned with the firm's new name: Lerner, Mitchell and Smith.

Holding one of the foil embossed business cards in her hand, Lina could feel the smile stretching across her face. Seeing her name in gold foil, free of any ties to her past, felt wonderful. This was a dream come true, and a moment many years in the making. She'd come from humble beginnings, worked hard to put herself through school and to prove herself as an attorney. Now, she'd finally landed her first partnership, and she couldn't be more ecstatic.

Wearing a broad smile of her own, Mrs. Lerner asked, "How does it feel, honey?"

"I've got to say, it feels pretty damn good. Thanks again for trusting me with the partnership, Gwen."

"I have the utmost faith in you, Lina."

"And I'll make sure that faith isn't misplaced." She removed a box of business cards that had her name on them, as well as one box of each of the other stationery items, and stacked them atop her desk.

With a nod, Mrs. Lerner gathered the larger box and left the office, letting the door swing shut behind her.

After taking a few moments to switch out her old

business cards for the new ones, and to put the other stationery where it belonged, Lina returned to her seat behind the desk. For a moment, she just sat back in the chair and took in the magnitude of the moment. Not only was she now a partner in a well-reputed firm in the Queen City, her new title had come with a considerable bump in her salary. With the infusion of cash in her account, she'd be able to finally take a long overdue vacation. She wasn't sure where she wanted to go yet, but she knew it would be someplace warm and tropical.

She remembered the approaching auction, and her smile softened. She felt pretty confident that she'd be able to outbid Rashad for Monk's piano. She still had concerns about the wealthy widow who'd been present at the first auction, though. The mysterious older woman seemed to be very well-off financially, and seemed to want the piano just as much as she and Rashad. There was no way to know how much the widow was willing to spend, and Lina knew there was a chance both she and Rashad might be outbid, and lose the chance to possess the piano. There was also the matter of the call-in bidder, she wasn't even sure if that bid had ever been verified.

Her thoughts shifted from the auction back to Rashad. Friday night, he'd shown her passion like she'd never experienced with anyone else. Those hours of hot, body-shaking loving had all been brought on by his determination to prove his devotion to her. The memories of his loving had stayed with her throughout the weekend. After all he'd given her, she definitely believed him. Now there would be no more lip from her about his so-called groupies, because he'd made it crystal clear where his affections lay.

And now that she knew just how he felt, she couldn't help relaxing the vice-like grip she usually kept on her emotions. He'd managed to soften her, and now she knew it would only be a matter of time before she admitted to him that she'd fallen for him. As a cautious woman by nature, though, she'd try to hold on to her heart as long as she could.

The buzzing of her phone interrupted her thoughts. She picked it up from the tray she kept it in on the edge of the desk and glanced at the screen. Seeing who it was, she answered with a smile. "Hey, Mama. How are you feeling today?"

"Pretty good, and from the sound of your voice, so are you."

She rolled her eyes. Her mother could always pick up on her emotions. "I'm doing great, Mama. Mrs. Lerner just brought in the new stationery for the firm, listing me as partner. It's gorgeous—linen paper, gold embossed, very executive."

"Congratulations again, baby. I always knew you'd get the recognition you deserved."

"Thanks, Mama."

There was a brief pause before Carla spoke again. "But that's not what's really got you so happy, is it?"

Lina let her eyes close for a moment. Her mother's perceptiveness could be a thorn in her side at times. "Mama."

"Don't Mama me. I know exactly what's going on. Things are getting serious with Rashad, aren't they?

I told you before he's a good man. You'd better stake your claim before other prospects start sniffing around him."

She chuckled. "You mean gold diggers, Mama?"

"Whatever. All I'm saying is you'd better make it clear he's yours."

"I got it, Mama."

"You'd better. I'm not trying to be in your business but you know it's rare you get a second chance with a man like that."

Lina giggled. She loved the way her mother always claimed not to be involved in her personal life, in the same breath told her just what she should do about it. Carla's newfound interest in her relationship status was very telling. "Okay, Mama. I hear you. I'm going to take you for a spa day to celebrate my promotion, so go ahead and decide what services you want." If things went well, she'd be able to let Mama know while they were enjoying a mud bath that she was the proud owner of Monk's piano.

"That's nice, Lina. But I know you are trying to change the subject."

*Busted.* Lina chuckled. "Can you blame me? But seriously, we are going to the spa."

"Mmm-hmm."

Lina knew that if she didn't get her mother off the phone, she'd never get her work done. "I've gotta go, I need to finish some work. Are you good on all your pills?"

"Yes. I'll need a refill on one of them next week, though."

"I'll make sure you get it. Love you."

"Love you, too, baby."

Lina disconnected the call and returned her phone to the tray. She yawned, doing her best to shake off the distracting thoughts of Rashad, and her mother's insistent advice on making things official with him. The contract she'd been reading wasn't going to evaluate itself, so she pulled the pages back out and spread them atop her desk. There were still two hours left in the workday, and despite her emotions being all over the place due to Rashad and her new title, she wanted to make them as productive as she could.

Taking a deep breath, she dove back into her work.

Rashad strolled into the register of deeds office Tuesday morning, whistling. The weather outside was delightful, traffic had been pretty light for rush hour in Charlotte and he'd just gotten a sexy good-morning text from Lina. Aside from that, today was the day he would put his plan to help Rick into action. All in all, the day was off to an awesome start.

As he moved through the main area of the office, past the cubicles of his employees, he paused to greet the folks who'd already come in for the day. There were still thirty-five or so minutes until the office officially opened for business, so a few people hadn't yet arrived.

His cheery demeanor didn't go unnoticed, nor was it contagious. Everyone spoke, but hardly anyone smiled and he got a few strange looks from some of the workers. Shrugging it off, he made his way down the narrow corridor toward the three offices in the back.

Juggling a cup of coffee and his keys, he fiddled around until he got the door to his office unlocked, then opened it and stepped inside. Within a few minutes, he was set up at his desk and ready to take on the day's tasks.

The first couple of hours of the day were filled with phone calls, answering emails and approving various pieces of paperwork. The eleven o'clock hour rolled around, and Rashad got up from the desk to stretch, hoping to loosen the tightness that had developed in his neck and shoulders from being tied to the desk all morning.

Just as he sat down, his boss walked in through the open door. "Are you busy, Rashad?"

He shook his head. "Just taking a little break. What can I do for you?"

Gary's expression was grim. "I've just got some news from the county."

"Your face says the news isn't good. More cutbacks?"

A nod was Gary's reply.

He sighed. "Okay. Who's being let go this time?"

"You are. I'm sorry, Rashad."

Hearing that news took the wind right out of his sails. "Seriously?"

"The commissioner says that in this type of economy, I don't have the luxury of employing two assistant RODs. They're keeping Kaye because she's paid a lot less than you are."

Rashad leaned back in his chair, not sure of how to react. "Well, this sucks. I'd planned to resign today, in hopes of the budget for my salary going toward keeping Rick Havens on, at least for a few months."

Gary wrung his hands, as he tended to do in stressful situations. "Again, I'm sorry. My hands are tied here."

"I know it's not your fault, Gary."

"Good news is, they've agreed to pay three months' severance pay and benefits."

Rashad's ears perked up, and he sat forward in his chair. "I've got an idea. Tell county that I'll resign my position, but only if they transfer my severance package to Rick Havens."

Gary's brow knitted. "That's awfully generous of you, man. Are you sure about this?"

"Yes. I don't really need it, I've got some cash stashed away. And since I make about double what Rick did, the package should set him up nicely for the next six months or so. County won't try to stop me from doing this, will they?"

Gary shook his head. "They can't. State and federal law says you can do whatever you want with your severance package."

"In that case, this is what I want to do. See to it that Rick Havens gets it all."

Standing, Gary stuck out his hand. "Rashad, you're a stand-up guy. I really respect you for doing this. Let me get the paperwork and we'll set it in motion."

He shook hands with his boss. "If things have to be this way, I'm just glad I can still do something to help Rick out. He's a good guy."

A few minutes later, Rashad sat alone in his office.

He felt some degree of sadness at the loss of his job, but that was overridden by all the good feelings he was experiencing. He'd done right by Rick, and now Rick could do right by his grandchildren. Being able to give a good friend peace of mind was a wonderful feeling, and he couldn't wait to see the look on Rick's face when he found out.

He looked around at his degree, the pictures of his favorite jazz artists and the music memorabilia he'd collected over the years. On the wall there was framed sheet music, an original Playbill from the single run of *Sophisticated Ladies* on Broadway, a few articles that had been written about the Gents in regional newspapers and magazines. All the things that made this office his were about to be boxed up and taken away. He'd put in eleven years with the register of deeds office, and he'd come to enjoy his work despite the stigma of civil service and the sometimes unpleasant attitudes of coworkers and citizens alike. Now it was about to be over, and he had to admit that he would miss it.

What was most important to him was that he'd done the best job he could during his time there, and that he'd kept his word to Rick Havens. He would bet that anyone else he'd had dealings with during his time there would agree that he was a man of his word. Hard work and honesty would be his legacy, and that was nothing to be ashamed of. It reflected the solid values his parents had instilled in him as a boy, and he would look back on these years with pride.

Deciding not to put off the inevitable, he left the

office in search of a few boxes. When he returned, he started packing up some of his prized possessions. When Gary came in with the paperwork he'd spoken of earlier, Rashad took a few minutes to sign and initial in all the places indicated. With his signature at the bottom of the last page, his entire severance package was officially transferred to Rick.

"You won't have to vacate the office until the end of the week, you know." Gary stood by the door with the folder containing the forms, watching Rashad pack.

"I know. I'll hang around until then to make sure everything around here is squared away, but I'm going to take some things home today. If I take a little every day it won't be such a huge undertaking on my last day."

"Smart." Gary and the folder disappeared out the door.

His phone, tucked in the pocket of his slacks, vibrated against his hip. He took it out and read a text message from Lina.

How's your day going?

He tapped out a reply. Okay, but I just lost my job. The phone buzzed again with her response.

Sorry to hear that. Sounds like you could use some comfort.

Not one to turn down her company, he smiled and replied.

I could. Come over to my house tonight, around 7?

He went back to placing things into the large box on his desk. The phone buzzed again.

I'll be there.

Smiling, he tucked his phone away. Just the thought of seeing Lina tonight raised both his spirits and parts of his anatomy. He went back to packing, willing the day to pass quickly, because he couldn't wait to get his sexy lady back in his arms again.

# Chapter 11

"Here's one more." Lina passed the last dirty utensil to Rashad. She stood next to him at the sink in his well-stocked kitchen, helping with the dishes. He'd washed while she'd rinsed and dried, and now the task was almost complete.

His kitchen, like the rest of his home, hadn't changed much since she'd last been there, over six months ago. The decor was minimalist and practical throughout, and in no other room was that more evident than in his kitchen. It had all the modern appointments: black granite countertops flecked with gray and gold, black and white tiled floors, a center island with a set of gleaming stainless steel pots and pans suspended above it. All the appliances were black, from the French door refrigerator to the gas stove, and there wasn't a finger-print or smudge in sight.

While the place was kept pleasantly clean, it was obvious no woman lived in the house. There were no decorative towels, no throw rugs, and no place mats or linens to be seen. The only towel he had on display was the one she'd used to dry the dishes, and it was the same austere black-and-white pattern as the tile floor beneath her bare feet.

There was, however, a single piece of art hanging on the wall. Just above the small two-person table that occupied the back wall of the kitchen, situated between the garage door and the pantry, hung a framed collection of album covers. There were four of them, all full-size and full color, all anchored to the wall inside the same multiwindow, black lacquer frame. All were recordings by Thelonious Monk: *The Complete Blue Note Recordings*, *Blue Monk*, *'Round Midnight* and *Reflections*. She glanced over at them. Seeing them there only served as a reminder of the upcoming auction for the legendary piano.

He took the knife from her and tossed it into the orange scented, soapy water. "Thanks for helping with the dishes."

"No problem. Your fajitas were pretty damn good, it was the least I could do." After the long day she'd had at the law firm, she'd thoroughly enjoyed his cooking. The chicken had been well seasoned and accompanied by sweet peppers, onions, warm tortillas and an array of toppings. After feasting on the meal and enjoying an ice-cold bottle of Corona, she was both stuffed and relaxed.

She let her eyes sweep over him, and had to admit she was enjoying the view. His locks were banded together at his nape, the brown tips hanging past his broad shoulders. He wore a white tank top that clung to his muscular torso and revealed the full glory of his corded arms. As he scrubbed the dishes beneath the foamy surface of the water, she watched his biceps and triceps flex. She was so busy staring she didn't notice when he tried to hand her the clean fork.

"Lina." He snapped his fingers.

She jumped. "Yeah?"

"Dry this, baby." He dangled the fork in front of her.

"Sorry." Taking it, she grabbed the checked soft towel from the counter and dried off the utensil. Once she'd placed it in the stainless steel dish rack, she put the towel back on the hook.

When she turned around, he drew her into his arms. "Have I told you yet how much I appreciate you coming over?"

A smile stretched across her face. She found herself smiling all the time when she was with him. "Yes, but don't worry. I'm not tired of it yet."

He gifted her with a sweet kiss, just a brief brushing of his lips against hers.

As short as the kiss was, it was still enough to put fire in her blood. It didn't take much to crank up her desire, not where he was concerned. To keep the feeling from taking over and overriding her good sense, she spoke. "You know, I'm sorry about what happened to you, but I'm still going to try to outbid you for the piano."

He shrugged his shoulders, looking completely nonplussed. "I wouldn't expect anything less from you."

Her brow hitched, but she didn't say anything. Instead, she looked into his dark eyes and tried to figure out just what his game was. He'd just lost his source of income, yet he seemed just as confident as ever that he'd be able to win the bid for the piano. Was this his version of a poker face, or was he sitting on some stash she knew nothing about? There was no way for her to tell by looking at him, and she certainly wasn't about to ask him. *Better to let him think I'm not worried about it.* So she fixed him with a stare just as cool and collected as his own.

His gaze drifted behind her, as if he were admiring his album cover collection. "Did you know that ''Round Midnight' is the most-recorded jazz standard in American history? Think of what that means about Monk as a composer. The most recorded standard in history is his—not Cole Porter, not Gershwin, not even the Duke."

"I didn't know that. It's very impressive." She watched the way his eyes lit up as he spoke. The passion he had for Monk's artistry, and for jazz in general, was very real and palpable. Standing in the circle of his arms, she realized that she wanted him to be just as passionate about her. If his lovemaking were any indication, he was already there. But could she trust him enough to give him the same in return?

"Without Monk, jazz as we know it wouldn't exist.

Bop, stride piano, he was the mastermind behind all of that. I can just imagine those early days when he played at Minton's up in Harlem with Dizzy, Charlie Parker and Miles Davis. Man that must have been something to hear."

"You're schooling me, I'll admit it. My mother is the real jazz fan. Even though I grew up listening to Monk's music, I don't know much about his life." She'd enjoyed the pianist's music, along with some of the other jazz greats who'd owned the scene from the '40s through the '60s. That was her mother's preferred era. As an adult, her musical taste was pretty eclectic. She listened to almost everything, except death metal and hardcore rap.

"That's why I'm going after the piano, baby. After years of admiring Monk, learning about him, studying his style, I feel like I knew him. He's been a big part of my life."

She couldn't really argue with him there. The influence Monk had on Rashad was undeniable. "I believe you. I don't really know whose cause is nobler, but I do want my mother to have the piano. I know it will go a long way toward raising her spirits, and seeing her happy is very important to me."

His open palm skimmed over her shoulder blade, trailing down her side until he got a firm grip on her ass. "I don't think we're going to solve this now. So why don't we put our time to good use."

Her breath hitched as he eased his hand lower, letting it slip beneath the hem of her knee-length sheath.

As his fingertips grazed up her bare hip, his name escaped her lips on a breathy sigh. "Rashad—"

He ventured farther, easing his hand around until he slid aside the thin swath of fabric between her thighs. Deftly he stroked her, lightly caressing that tiny kernel of flesh made only for pleasure. "I love to hear you say my name."

"Oh…" It was all she could manage to utter as one long finger dipped inside her, the tip curving forward against her G-spot. Her legs began to tremble as liquid heat pooled in her lower regions.

As if he sensed her instability, he edged her back a few steps until the small of her back came to rest against the island's granite top. His hand continued its magical ministrations, and her vision swam as her eyes began to cross, and then roll up inside her head.

"Come for me, baby. Call my name again." His deep voice touched her almost as potently as his hands.

Her head dropped back. His questing finger was joined by another, hotly stroking her insides until she melted into bliss. And just as he'd requested, she came for him, and screamed his name into the silence.

Rashad watched Lina intently, enjoying the sight of her laid out across his kitchen island. She made for quite an erotic sight—her pebbled nipples visible beneath the thin fabric of her dress, which was now pulled up around her waist. Her usually perfect hairdo was disheveled, and the rapid rise and fall of her chest matched her panting breaths. There was no other sight on earth to be compared with a woman in the afterglow of orgasm, and no other woman wore that glow as beautifully as Lina.

He eschewed thoughts of his lost job, of Monk's piano and everything else. Right now the only thing he cared about was getting as deep inside of her as possible, as quickly as possible.

He ran his open hand along the plane of her stomach, and she shivered. "Baby, can I—"

Her whispered answer came before he could even complete the question. "Yes. Make love to me, Rashad."

Needing no further encouragement, he knelt briefly to slide the soft blue bikini panties down her legs. Normally he would have undressed her fully, carried her to his bed. But the sight of her displayed on the island countertop had him so hard and so full of need, he knew he wouldn't make it that far. So once her panties were tossed aside, he fit himself between her open thighs.

She sat up, her eyes blazing with heat. Never breaking eye contact with him, she undid the button and zipper of his jeans. Apparently she wasn't interested in prolonging the encounter, either, because she reached inside his pants, wove her hand through the slit opening in his boxer briefs, and grasped his manhood.

He uttered a curse as her warm palm surrounded him, just the way he wanted her to. Her eyes still locked with his, she began to stroke him slowly, skillfully. The building pleasure gripped him, and he stayed her hand. "If you don't stop this will be over before it starts."

Complying, she ceased her sinfully delightful hand

game, but still pulled him free of his underwear. Bracing herself by resting her elbows on the countertop, she arched her back. "Let's get the party started, then."

He fished a condom from his pocket and covered himself in record time. His pants were still slung low on his hips, but he had neither time nor inclination to take them down. In the next heartbeat, he tilted his hips and slid inside her. They both gasped at the joining. He remained still for a minute. The residual pleasure she'd given him with her hand, combined with the hot tightness of her now, threatened to make him spill right away. Inhaling deeply, he took in the scent of her perfume and her arousal, then began to thrust.

Soft moans escaped her open mouth as he stroked her, his hands drifting over the peaks and valleys of her body. He used the pads of his thumbs to tease her erect nipples and she arched like a drawn bow. Behind him, he felt her long legs drape around his hips, and he moved his hands to her waist, bracing her for the passion he could no longer hold at bay.

Now his thrusts became deeper, harder and more powerful. The musical sounds of her moans increased in kind and it sounded sweeter than anything he'd ever heard. She was close to orgasm again, he could tell by the sight and sound of her. So he eased his hand between them and circled his thumb over her hot little clit. She yelled out his name, and he felt her body convulse around him.

Unable to hold back any longer, he growled as his own release spiraled through him.

When he came back to awareness, he let himself slip

free of her body's warmth and eased away to discard the condom. He tucked his member out of sight and fastened his jeans. Then he gathered her still shivering form in his arms and carried her into his bedroom.

Once there, he pulled back the covers and placed her beneath them. She was half-asleep, a sated smile gracing her beautiful face. He turned to sneak away, and her soft voice stopped him.

"Where are you going?"

"To take a shower. Just rest. I'll be back."

Seeming to accept his answer, she snuggled down in the bed and pulled the covers up around her chin. Before he reached his bathroom door, he heard her soft snores ruffling the silence.

Knowing he'd loved her thoroughly enough to put her to sleep pleased him. A smile stretched across his face as he entered his bathroom.

Moments later he stood beneath the steaming hot spray of water. Even as he washed away the sweat he worked up making love to her, and the scent of her clinging to skin, he knew there was no washing away his feelings. He loved her more than his next breath. She had to know that by now, but would she ever fully trust him? And could he really expect her to, since he hadn't told her about his family, and the arrangements they'd made for him?

He knew she would soon find out, because the time was fast approaching when he'd have no choice but to reveal everything. How would she react? As he watched the suds disappear down the drain, he realized she might not be happy about it all. Still, he had to bide his time. Telling her now was out of the question, so he would just have to wait and see how things turned out.

He emerged from the shower, clean and relaxed, to find her still sound asleep. Taking in the sight of her lying so peacefully in his bed, filled his heart. It was a welcome sight, one he would be more than happy to wake up to every morning for the rest of his life.

*Forever. How can I convince her to stay forever?*

He was taken aback by that thought. He'd never thought of any other woman this way. Had he really reached the point where he was ready for marriage? Maybe he had, because deep down he felt she belonged with him. He wanted her in his arms, in his bed, and in his life, always.

Once he'd toweled off and slipped into a clean pair of boxers, he lifted the covers and slid into bed beside her.

## Chapter 12

Lifting her feet up onto the plush leather ottoman in front of her, Lina sank down into the soft embrace of the matching armchair. She was sitting in a popular coffee shop, waiting for Eve to arrive. It was early evening, and she looked forward to seeing her best friend today. With all the cases and new responsibilities she'd been dealing with at work, she hadn't been left with much time to hang out with her friend. Being able to see her in the middle of the workweek was a rare treat.

The coffee shop's decor provided a perfect backdrop for enjoying a cup of Joe and good company. The muted color palate of soft grays, blues and greens, as well as the light classical music being piped in, made the space great for relaxation. Still, it was a coffee shop, which meant all the tables near a wall outlet were taken up by serious-looking folks eyeballing laptop and tablet screens. "Power zombies," as she called them, seemed to appear the moment the place opened, so they could secure an outlet and remain tethered to it all day. She hadn't a clue what the power zombies were working on, or even if they were working at all, but the sight of them tickled her.

She grabbed her iced coffee and took a sip, while flipping through the pages of a fashion magazine she'd picked up on the way in. It was a regional magazine called *Southern Sass,* and even though she'd never heard of it, she was impressed with the clothing and accessories displayed inside. All the items in the fashion spreads were made by designers and artisans who lived in the southeastern United States and she found it a very clever and well-executed publication.

"Hey, girl." Eve's greeting cut into her thoughts.

Lina looked up and watched as her friend flopped down in the chair across from her.

Right away, she noticed how tired Eve looked. Though she was as impeccably dressed as ever in a sunny-yellow maxidress and carrying an orange handbag, Eve's face was lined with exhaustion.

"Girl. What's going on with you? You look tired." Lina couldn't help asking the question. She'd never seen her friend like this before. Frankly, she felt concerned.

"I am tired. I haven't been sleeping that well lately." Eve stifled a yawn.

"You don't have a drink. Do you want me to get

you something, before you tell me what's got you lying awake at night?"

Eve chuckled. "Sure. Get me a decaf caramel mocha."

Lina nodded, then walked about two steps before she remembered. "Eve, you hate caramel. Are you sure that's what you want?"

Lying back in the chair, Eve replied, "I'm sure. I've had a taste for caramel lately."

Shaking her head, Lina walked up to the counter and ordered what her friend had asked for. When she returned with the steaming hot drink and handed it over, Lina sat back down in her own chair.

"You know, I've got some serious questions about why you're so tired, and why you suddenly like caramel, and why you're drinking that hot espresso when it's about a thousand degrees outside." Lina loved a good espresso as much as the next girl, but she couldn't stand drinking hot drinks during the long, humid Carolina summers.

Taking a long sip from the mug, Eve fixed her with that famous side-eye. "If you think about everything you just said for a minute, I think you'll be able to figure it out."

Lina crossed her legs and leaned forward. Through narrowed eyes, she watched Eve, who seemed content to half sit, half lie in her chair drinking her beverage. A few seconds ticked by in silence.

Eve smiled.

Lina jumped up from her seat. "Oh my God. You're pregnant!"

Her smile widening, Eve nodded. "Ding, ding, ding! Give the lady a prize."

Giving Eve a moment to set her mug aside, Lina held open her arms and hugged her friend tight. "Girl, I'm so happy for you. So happy."

Returning the hug, Eve laughed. "I'm happy, too. So quit squeezing me before you make me have to go pee again."

They broke the embrace and returned to their seats. Lina asked, "What about Darius? When did you tell him? How did he take the news?"

A dreamy look washed over Eve's face. "I found out last week, after the book club meeting. I told him that night, and for a minute I thought he was going to faint. But he was so sweet. He got down on his knees and kissed my belly."

"Aw!" There was really nothing else she could say.

"I went to the doctor yesterday, and they say I'm due around the second week of December."

Lina couldn't stop smiling. Knowing that her friend would achieve her lifelong dream of motherhood had her grinning ear to ear. "I'm sorry you'll have to carry the baby through a North Carolina summer, but I'm so happy for you. Wow."

"Wow is right. I'm still adjusting to it. And now I'm going to have to figure out who's going to run things at FTI when I go on maternity leave. I want to take off at least six months."

"Who knows? You may fall in love with the baby and never want to go back."

Eve shrugged. "We'll see. That would really be

something, after all I went through to get the CEO position." She fell silent.

Lina instinctively knew that talking about FTI and the baby had probably made Eve think of her late father, Joseph. Franklin Technologies, Incorporated was Eve's software company, and represented Joseph's legacy. She sensed the cloud of sadness that had descended over Eve. Without a word, she got up and went to sit next to her. It was going to be a tight fit, but to comfort her best friend, a little discomfort would be well worth it. Wedging her hips in next to Eve, she took her friend into her arms.

"I know you miss him, girl. Trust me, he's watching from above. Everything is going to be okay."

Eve sniffled, sighed. "Logically I know that. But these hormones have got me all emotional."

She grew quiet again, and Lina didn't press her to talk. Instead, she just held her friend, while the wordless tears rolled down her cheeks. Lina had been there when Eve's father had passed less than a year ago. Time had eased her pain, but the loss still hurt. Lina understood. It had been more than a decade since she'd lost her own father, and she still shed tears for him now and then. The loss of a father was something a daughter never really got over. After all, a father is the first man to win his daughter's heart.

Once the tears subsided, Eve straightened up. She dabbed at her eyes with a napkin, took a deep breath. "I think I'm okay now. Thanks, Lina."

"No problem. Just doing my best friend duty." She wriggled from the tight spot between Eve's hip and the arm of the chair and stood, before easing back into her own chair. Mentally, she made a note of all the people she'd need to call to start planning a baby shower. There was no way she was going to let her best friend step into motherhood without a big celebration, and she knew all the girls from the book club would agree.

"You should have seen the look on Mom's face when I told her. She is so excited about having a grandchild, she doesn't know what to do with herself."

Lina giggled. "Has she already told you what you should name the baby?"

Joining in her laughter, Eve nodded. "Of course she has. If it's a girl, I'm to name the baby after her, and if it's a boy, I'm to name it after Daddy."

"I'm not sure. Louise and Joseph are kind of old-fashioned names. Now, Lina, that has a nice, modern ring to it."

Eve rolled her eyes dramatically. "Girl, please. I'm sure between Darius and me, we can come up with a name."

"I guess I can accept that. Okay then, you and your husband have my permission to name your own child."

That snarky remark sent both of them into peals of laughter. The two of them had been thick as thieves since college, and that was precisely why they understood each other.

Eve's expression changed, as if she'd just remembered something. "Enough about me. I want to hear what's been going on with you and Rashad."

At the mere mention of Rashad's name, Lina felt the sweet warmth of desire flow through her body like a charge of electricity. A soft smile tugged at her lips. "Things are going great. He's attentive, affectionate and he cooks."

"Really? Sounds like things are getting pretty serious between you two."

"I think they are. He got laid off over at the courthouse last week, so I went over there to hang out with him. I thought he would be upset, but he seems to be taking it all in stride."

Eve cocked a brow. "You went over to his house? You haven't been there in ages. How did that go?"

"We watched TV for a while, and he made me the most awesome chicken fajitas…"

Eve pursed her lips. "Girl, bye. You know good and well what I'm asking about. Did he handle his business or what?"

Wondering if the "hormones" had increased Eve's nosiness, Lina shook her head. Heat rose into her face as she quietly admitted, "We made love on his kitchen counter."

"Girl!" Eve moved to the edge of her seat. "Details!"

Lina shushed her. "I'm not trying to put all my business in the streets, so lower your voice."

"Whatever. I'll be quieter, just tell me everything."

So Lina leaned in and whispered the racy details of her sexy kitchen encounter with Rashad into her friend's ear. By the time she was done, both of them were giggling like two adolescents.

"I didn't know Rashad had it like that." Eve looked genuinely impressed.

"Neither did I. mean, his lovemaking game was

good when we dated before, but now…the brother's got his PhD in making me scream." Lina smacked her lips as she remembered the mind-blowing pleasure he'd given her.

"I bet you're glad he studied up." Eve winked.

As Lina drained the last of her iced coffee, she smiled, because she had to agree.

Reaching for the handle of his tennis racket, Rashad removed it from his duffel bag and gave it a mock swing. It was beautiful Thursday. The early afternoon sun beamed down on the textured green surface of the tennis court at his housing complex, radiating heat back toward him. Dressed in white shorts and Carolina blue polo shirt, he felt pretty comfortable despite the near ninety-degree temperature.

He glanced beyond the fence surrounding the court, searching for any sign of his relatives. His parents and younger sister had arrived in town last night, and were due to stay in Charlotte for several days. Rashad's father, Vernon, owned a furniture manufacturing company in their hometown of Chattanooga, and was in town on business. Rashad's mother, Gladys, and sister, Simone, had decided to accompany Vernon in order to get in some overdue family bonding time.

Despite his insistence that they save a little money and stay in the two spare rooms in his place, Rashad's family members were all staying in a hotel downtown. His father had called him up after breakfast with the idea that they all meet for a doubles tennis match, something they'd enjoyed doing back home when Rashad and his sister were younger. Rashad had agreed and invited them all over to use the court just down the road from his home. There were several municipal courts around the city, but this one was so close by, and was also kept in near immaculate condition by the complex staff.

Taking out his tube of tennis balls, he removed one. Bouncing it a few times on the court, he took a step back and executed a powerful underhand swing. The racket sliced through the air, totally missing the ball, which bounced once more before rolling under the net.

"I hope you'll do better than that during the actual game," a deep and familiar voice chided.

Rolling his eyes, Rashad turned toward the sound. "Hey, Dad. How are you?"

Dressed in khaki shorts and a bright white polo shirt, Vernon MacRae strode through the open gate and onto the court. "Pretty good. How have you been, son?"

Grabbing his father in a customary bear hug, he chuckled. "I'm good. And yes, I plan to do better during the game."

"Don't make it too easy for us, bro." Simone strolled onto the court behind Vernon. She'd pulled her hair up into a ponytail and donned a lavender tennis dress and matching sneakers. The diamond-encrusted treble clef that she never took off hung from the gold chain around her neck.

Rashad gave Simone a playful slap on the back, then kissed her forehead. He reached out to rumple her hair, but the pursed lips and side-eye she gave him made him change his mind. At twenty-six, she was a full decade younger than him, and often complained that having him as a big brother felt like having two fathers. Because he loved her, Rashad ignored her whining. Any older brother worth his salt would do his best to protect his baby sister. Besides, they had no other siblings, so he felt a special sense of responsibility for her.

Moving past her, he greeted his mother. The huge black-framed sunglasses she wore hid much of her face. Still, it was easy to tell that behind the dark lenses, her eyes were plastered to the screen of her smartphone. "Hey, Mom. How are you?"

Gladys looked up, offering him a smile and a kiss on the cheek. "Doing just fine."

Simone smacked her lips. "Mom, get off Twitter so we can play."

"Oh, hush, girl." But Gladys complied with her daughter's request, turning off the screen. She then pocketed the phone on the hip of her tennis skirt.

By now, Vernon had his racket in hand. "Let's get this game underway, shall we?"

After some maneuvering, the usual teams were formed. Rashad and Vernon stood on one side of the net, while Simone and Gladys stood on the other. Simone gave the first serve, bouncing the ball in front of her before giving a swing that sent it sailing over the net, right toward Vernon's head.

Vernon ducked instinctively, but before the ball could hit him, Rashad made a leap in his direction and swiped the ball back toward their opponents.

"Trying to kill your old man, Simone?"

"Sorry, Dad!" Simone shouted as Gladys returned the ball.

The game went on for over an hour, with them smacking the ball back and forth over the net. There were a few times the ball flew off course and either Rashad or Simone went after it. By the time it ended, the ladies emerged victorious, but everyone had worked up a good sweat.

Rashad dropped onto one of the metal benches just outside the court's fence, dragging a towel from his duffel over his forehead.

His father sat next to him, wiping off his own perspiration. "I thought you said you were gonna do better during the game."

Chuckling, Rashad tucked the towel back into his bag. "Don't tease me, Dad. I'm distracted."

"I can tell. What's got you so unfocused, boy?"

He thought of Lina, remembering the way she'd looked, half-naked and draped over his kitchen island. While the memory was as vivid and sweet as could be, he knew better than to tell his father all that. "Let's just say Lina's back in my life, and things are going well."

Vernon gave him a hearty slap on the back. "Good, good! It's about time."

Simone and Gladys strolled over. Simone had both her own bag and her mother's slung over her shoulder. "What are y'all talking about?"

"Rashad's back with Lina," Vernon volunteered.

One of Simone's perfectly arched brows hitched up. "Oh, really? So you're back with Miss I-Don't-Trust-Nobody. When did this happen?"

Before Rashad could answer, the loud grumbling of his stomach interrupted his thoughts. "Look, y'all can grill me all you want, but let's do it over lunch. I'm starving."

Everyone agreed, so they returned to Rashad's house. He and his father went to separate bathrooms to take a quick shower while his mom and sister prepped for lunch. Then they switched, with the women getting their showers while the men finished up the cooking.

By the time everybody was clean and freshly dressed, Rashad had set the table. With his parents and sister seated around the polished black lacquer table, he set out the bowls and platters holding the meal. There were large leaves of bib lettuce, grilled chicken and steak and jasmine rice, as well as sesame oil, teriyaki sauce, and chopped scallions for toppings. The Asian lettuce wraps had always been a favorite dish around the MacRae household, and Rashad usually made them for his family whenever they visited.

Once grace was said and the platter passed around, Gladys launched right into the topic at hand. "So, how long have you and Miss Lina been seeing each other?"

Rashad thought back to the night he'd run into Lina at Cleveland and Wendell. "It's been a little less than two weeks."

Gladys sipped from her glass of ice water. "That's it? How can you already be so sure things are going to be better this go-round?"

Chewing a mouthful of food, Rashad contemplated his answer. He dared not tell his mother just how "close" he and Lina had gotten over the past couple of weeks, so he chose his words carefully. "Instinctively, I can sense her opening up to me and trusting me in a way she couldn't before."

Simone scoffed, but said nothing.

Rashad cut his eyes at his sister, wondering why she had such an attitude when it came to Lina. After all, the two of them had never met.

Vernon, who up until that moment had seemed content to listen and fill his belly, spoke. "Does she know about your 'backup plan' yet?"

As three sets of curious eyes regarded him, Rashad shook his head. "No. I don't want to tell her until it's absolutely necessary. You all know how women have reacted to finding out about it in the past, so I decided to just play it close to the vest this time."

Clamping her hand over her mouth, Simone faked a cough.

Rashad turned to her. "Is there a piece of steak caught in your throat or something, Simone?"

She shook her head, but her tight-lipped expression was telling.

"If you've got something to say, say it."

She shook her head again. "Nope. I'm not getting in the middle of this."

That made him chuckle. His sister never had any qualms about getting in his business before. But if she claimed disinterest, he wasn't about to press her.

Vernon interjected. "Well, I hope she takes it well and behaves accordingly. The good news is profits are way up at MacRae Incorporated, so..." He gestured with his hands.

Rashad understood the implications of his father's words right away. "That's good to hear, Dad."

"And since you're not working at the courthouse anymore, you're free to come back anytime."

He knew that. His father had made it abundantly clear that he'd always be welcome to take on an executive role at MacRae Incorporated. But they both knew that the family manufacturing business wasn't Rashad's dream. What he wanted was a regular job, a regular life, lived amongst regular people. "I'll think about it."

Vernon rested his elbows on the table, lacing his fingers together. "I know your grandfather soured you on our lifestyle, Rashad. But you're always welcome to come home."

Not wanting to think about his grandfather's selfish, condescending ways, Rashad offered only an affirmative bob of his head in response. Solomon MacRae had shown him all the ways money could darken a person's soul, and Rashad's mission in life was to be as different from his grandfather as possible.

Rashad slid his chair back, rose from the table. "I lost my appetite."

Feeling his family's concerned gazes on his back, he left the room.

# Chapter 13

It was just past six when Lina pulled her car into the driveway at Rashad's condo Thursday evening. The garage doors were shut, and she assumed both spaces were occupied by Rashad's truck and whatever vehicle his parents drove. Cutting off the engine, she got out of the car but left the driver's door open. She dragged her purse onto the seat and fished out her travel-size lint roller. She took the gadget to her black slacks one more time, just to be sure no renegade fuzz had been missed when she'd done it earlier. Tucking the lint roller away, she looked in her side-view mirror at her reflection. Adjusting the shimmery gold one-shoulder top to just the right angle, she then ran a hand over her hair to be sure it was in place. After one more swipe of rose-gold lip gloss, she deemed herself presentable.

She slung the strap of her black leather satchel over her shoulder and shut the car door. While she walked up the short sidewalk, she contemplated on why she felt so nervous. Likely, it was because it had been years since a man had introduced her to his parents. Beyond that, Rashad didn't talk much about his family, so she had no idea what they were like. She knew she'd be meeting both his parents and his only sibling, but other than that, she didn't know what to expect.

She took a deep breath, blowing it out through her lips as she pressed the doorbell. The chime played for about two seconds before the door swung open.

The heady, masculine scent of Rashad's cologne wafted out the door and into her nostrils, as the sight of him standing there took her breath away. She knew she should speak, but she couldn't. All her brain space was currently occupied with drinking in his dark handsomeness. His locks were in a ponytail at his nape. He'd apparently gotten his left ear pierced, because there was a large round stud sparkling there. The suit he wore was tan, and must have been custom cut to fit his tall, muscular frame. He'd eschewed a tie, choosing instead to wear a crisp white button-down shirt beneath his sport coat, with the top three buttons undone.

He descended the single step, his dark brown loafers coming within an inch of her gold open-toed sandals. "Baby, you look gorgeous." He draped his arms around her waist, and gave her a soft kiss on the cheek.

His touch seemed to break the stupor she'd fallen

in when he opened the door, and she smiled up at him. "Thanks for having me over. You clean up pretty well yourself."

The dazzling smile that crossed his face was accompanied by a chuckle. "I'm glad you like it."

"Are you sure you still want to do this? Introducing me to your parents is a big step. They might think you're serious about me." She winked, not bothering to hide the teasing in her tone.

He grasped her hand, tugging her inside. "Good, because I *am* serious about you. Come on inside."

She followed him and he closed the door behind them. Still cradling her hand in his own, he led her straight through the living room and kitchen, and into the formal dining room. There, seated around the table, were his three family members.

She smiled and shook hands with them as Rashad introduced his mother, father and younger sister. His parents wore welcoming smiles, but his sister's expression was flat and unreadable. She could immediately see the resemblance between Rashad and Vernon, and she had to admit that the older man was somewhat of a silver fox. He wore both his dark suit and his salt-and-pepper beard with confidence.

Gladys MacRae was the picture of refinement. Her hair was fully gray but perfectly coiffed in a short natural style, and she wore a cream-colored skirt and a white blouse. Her gold jewelry was elegant and understated, as was her greeting.

Simone, the youngest MacRae, was the spitting image of her mother. She wore a pair of boot cut jeans and a navy silk blouse. Her long, jet-black hair was straightened and tucked into a demure bun. Lina complimented Simone on her makeup. The girl had a mean smoky eye and a vampy shade of burgundy lipstick that was to die for. Simone accepted the compliment with a quiet "thank you" and a Mona Lisa smile.

Rashad pulled out her chair, then took his seat next to her at one end of the table. Five places had been set with china plates, silverware, a filled champagne flute and a goblet of ice water. She noticed how nicely the table was set, and recalled the night several months ago when he'd invited her over for a candlelight dinner. That night was the last time she'd seen the linen napkins and gleaming crystal set before her now. That had also been the first time they'd made love. Thinking of the passion they'd shared that night, and of the ecstasy he'd been showing her these past sixteen days, made the heat rise into her face. She eased her chair closer to the table, hoping no one noticed the hitch in her breath.

Once everyone was seated, Lina unfolded her white linen napkin and placed it across her lap. When she looked up again, she noted that Vernon and Gladys were carrying on a quiet conversation, but Simone's searching eyes had never left her face.

Offering her a small smile, Lina turned to Rashad. "What's on the menu tonight, Rashad?"

The flame of passion dancing in his dark eyes told her that he wanted her on the table. He held her gaze as he spoke. "Surf and turf. I made ribeye steaks, steamed lobster tails, baked potatoes and salad."

"Wow. You're spoiling me." She reached over to clasp his hand.

Gladys emitted a tinkling laugh. "Well, aren't you two sweet together."

Rashad squeezed her hand. With his fiery gaze still locked on Lina, he said, "Sweeter than you could ever imagine."

A shiver shot through her body, because she knew what he was referring to. She agreed. What they'd shared was meaningful, erotic and fulfilling. Remembering the company she was in, she held tight to her composure.

Rashad and his father excused themselves and left the table. When Lina turned confused eyes to Gladys, the older woman smiled.

"That's how it's always been around our house. Vernon's always waited on us, and I suppose Rashad just picked up the habit from his father."

Before Lina could respond, the men returned with covered platters and serving utensils. The food was passed around family-style, and before long, she was sinking her teeth into one of the most flavorful meals she'd had in a long time. She was careful to mind her manners, wanting to make a good impression on his sister, but the food was so delicious it took a bit of extra effort.

She'd just swallowed a bite of lobster meat when she felt the dribble of melted butter run down her chin. She immediately reached for her napkin.

But before she could get it to her mouth, Rashad leaned over and kissed her, the tip of his tongue whisking away the butter, along with a small portion of her self-control. The task complete, he eased away and turned his attention back to his plate.

Vernon cleared his throat. "You know, Rashad has never introduced any woman he's dated, and I think I can see why."

Though she remained silent, the expression on Gladys's face conveyed her approval.

She could feel her cheeks heating up with embarrassment. "Sorry, Mr. MacRae."

He waved her off. "Nonsense, there's no reason to apologize. I'm glad to see my son feeling passionately about you. Up until now I didn't know if he could be passionate about anything other than singing and playing the piano."

Hearing that only made her blush more, but she also felt a measure of flattery. Everything she'd experienced and observed tonight led her to believe his parents liked her and approved of their relationship. There was still the matter of his younger sister. Looking over at Simone now, Lina found her expression just as unreadable as before.

As if she sensed her attention, Simone said, "If he's happy, I'm happy. I just hope you can get past your trust issues and give him a real shot this time."

Lina's eyes closed briefly. She could tell by Simone's tone that she simply didn't want her brother to get hurt, understandably so. Lina couldn't really blame Simone for acting as she did, it was plain to see that she loved her big brother. "I'll admit that I'm not perfect, and that

I've got some baggage. But I'll do the best I can to keep things kosher between me and Rashad. Fair enough?"

Simone gave a slow nod, finally letting a smile peek through. "Deal."

Beneath the table, Rashad rested his open palm on her thigh.

When their eyes connected, he smiled. And as she looked at him, she felt her heart thumping in her chest, and knew that the war was over.

She loved him, and there was no escaping it.

The morning sunlight streamed through the vertical blinds, casting lines of light on the hardwood floors of the den. Rashad stood in the middle of the floor, looking around the room as he tried to work out which spot would be best to place Monk's legendary gilded piano. Winning the bid was a foregone conclusion, even if no one knew it but him, so he'd have to take delivery on it. Knowing that, he wanted to make sure the space was cleared so the process of getting the piano into his possession could go as smoothly as possible.

Lately he'd been thinking a lot about the piano, and what he would do with it once he had it. If he kept it, he obviously wouldn't play it. He had a much more modern black baby grand in one of his spare rooms. To risk damaging a treasure like the Monk piano would be outrageous. If he kept it, he would simply display it, availing himself of the opportunity to look at it whenever he wanted.

He used his hand to cup his chin, wondering why what had formerly been a sure thing, was now an if.

Deep down, he knew why. As much as he wanted the piano, he knew Lina wanted it, too. That hadn't been an issue before, when he'd been so sure he was the more deserving party. As time went by, and he'd fallen deeper in love with her, he'd realized things were far more complicated than that. He loved Lina, both body and soul, he was way past the point of denying that. While his mind told him to get his hands on that piano and never let it go, his heart told him to do what would make her happy. As it stood now, he couldn't come up with a feasible way to keep the piano *and* make her happy.

*So I guess I have to decide what's more important to me.*

He was still standing in the center of the room, contemplating, when Simone walked in.

"What are you doing?" She padded barefoot across the floor and settled on the white leather love seat.

He shrugged. "I thought I was trying to pick out a spot for Monk's piano, but now I don't know what the hell I'm doing."

"Don't tell me you're worried about winning the bid."

"No, that's not it." He ran a hand over his hair.

"What's the problem then, bro?"

"I didn't mention it to you and Mom and Dad before, but Lina is bidding on the piano, too."

Simone cocked a brow. "She's a Monk fan? Even if she is, I've never known one to geek out for him like you."

He rolled his eyes at his sister's remark. "No, she's

not a Monk fan, her mother is. She wants the piano as a gift for her mother."

"That's noble and all, but we both know you'll easily outbid her."

Rashad sighed. "We know that, but Lina doesn't."

Simone shifted in her seat, tucking her feet beneath her. "I know you have your reasons for not telling her about your backup plan and all, but you do know the feathers are about to hit the fan, right?"

"Maybe, maybe not. It all depends on how she takes the news."

"Ha! After the way she acted the last time you dated, do you really think there's a scenario where this isn't going to go badly for you? You said yourself she had serious trust issues, and you've essentially been lying to her the whole time you've known her."

"C'mon, Simone. I didn't lie to her about it, I just didn't tell her."

Simone sucked her teeth, folding her arms over her chest. "C'mon, nothing. You're talking to a woman here, and as a woman, I'm telling you. We consider omission to be just as much of a lie as fabrication, sir."

"I don't see it that way," he groused.

"Doesn't matter how you see it. From her perspective, you legit lied to her. And when she finds out, trust me, she isn't going to be happy about it."

He pressed his open palm into his face. "Shit."

Simone nodded. "Yeah, bro. You got serious problems."

"Well what am I supposed to do now? How do I handle this?"

She shrugged. "There's not a whole lot you can do, since you can't go back in time and be honest with her from the beginning. At this point, you just have to roll with it. Once you win the bid and she finds out, let her take the lead and just go with what she wants."

"What if what she wants is to never speak to me again?"

Simone's eyes held sympathy as she answered. "Then respect her enough to honor her wishes."

He sank down into the cushion of the matching armchair across from his sister, as his heart sank down into his slippers. As much as he and his friends complained about the absurd nature of female logic, he knew his sister was probably right. He was going to have to choose between Lina and the piano. And since the auction was tonight, he wouldn't have long to make his choice.

Thankfully, when he looked at it honestly, it wasn't that hard of a decision.

"You going to be okay, Rashad?" Simone's voice held notes of concern.

"I'll be fine. I just need to make a choice, and it may just be the most important decision of my life."

"I don't know if it's that serious. I know how much you idolize Monk, but it's just a piano."

"It's much more than that, Simone. It's my future."

Because when it came right down to it, he'd lived his whole life without even knowing Monk's piano existed, and it hadn't had any effect whatsoever on his life.

Yet, knowing Lina had changed his life irreversibly, he didn't want a future that didn't include her by his side.

# Chapter 14

When Cleveland and Wendell opened its doors for the first auction in two weeks, Lina was one of the first people in line. As the black-suited attendant handed her a paddle, he stepped aside so she could enter. Lina made a beeline for the auction room, doing her best to ignore the swarm of people entering directly behind her.

The moment she stepped into the room, she recalled the last time she'd been there. Her eyes naturally drifted to the spot at the back of the room where she'd laid eyes on Rashad in all his handsome glory. A smile touched her lips as she thought back on his determination to talk to her in spite of her outright disdain. Though she'd been annoyed with him that night, now she couldn't be gladder he'd ignored her protests.

The past two weeks had been such a whirlwind, she felt she was still catching up with herself.

People started to file in past her, making her realize she still stood in the center of the aisle. She took her seat on the left side of the aisle, the same front row seat she'd taken up last time. Looking around the room, she saw a familiar face: the wealthy older woman who'd bid on the piano the last time. She mulled it over for a few moments before she remembered the woman's last name, Parker.

Offering Mrs. Parker a congenial nod, Lina settled into the burgundy cushion and waited for the auction to begin. With any luck, Rashad wouldn't show up tonight. She didn't have any ill will for him, her blossoming love for him precluded that. But she really didn't relish the idea of embarrassing him when she outbid him for the piano. The man had already lost his job, and even though he seemed to be taking it well, she had to assume his ego had taken a hit. He'd shown her a pretty impressive bluff when she mentioned that she'd still do her best to outbid him. That didn't change the fact that it was very likely that either she or Mrs. Parker would be leaving there tonight with Monk's piano.

Most of the early birds were already in their seats, and she did her best to keep her eyes toward the raised platform at the front of the room. Even though the auction wasn't due to begin for another half hour or so, she didn't want to miss anything.

Nevertheless, the instant Rashad entered the room, her head swiveled around to look behind her. It was as if she were subconsciously aware of him before she ever caught sight of him. She watched him stroll up the center aisle, looking as delicious as ever in a pair of navy slacks and royal blue button-down shirt. His eyes were obscured by a pair of dark sunglasses. He'd left his locks unbound tonight, and for whatever reason, seeing his hair swinging free around his shoulders did something to her. She tugged down the hem of her green cocktail dress, crossing her legs in response to the tingle making its way up the insides of her thighs.

He caught her gaze, that easy smile spreading across his face. Walking toward her, he took off his sunglasses and tucked them away in the front pocket of his shirt. There was an empty seat next to her, and she realized now that she'd basically marked it for him by putting her purse there. She moved her bag out of the way just as he stopped in front of her.

"Hey, baby. You're looking radiant as always." He eased into the chair next to her and placed a soft kiss against her cheek.

Unable to resist, she let her fingertips play through the length of his hair. "Laying it on a little thick tonight, aren't you? I'm still going to try to win the bid, Rashad."

"Like I said, I wouldn't expect anything less from you." Appearing as nonplussed as ever, he leaned back in his chair and crossed his long legs at the ankle.

She shook her head. He certainly was skilled at keeping his aloof facade intact. Hopefully he'd react in a similar cool manner when she won the bidding.

She didn't say anything else, and neither did Rashad,

because the auctioneer had stepped up on the platform and approached the podium.

With his left arm still in a plaster cast, the older man looked a little worse for wear but seemed happy to be back to his job. "Ladies and gentlemen, welcome to Cleveland and Wendell. I'm pleased to be on the mend and back at the podium, so let's get started, shall we?"

A smattering of subdued applause filled the space as the wealthy patrons in the room expressed their agreement.

"At the last auction, there was some rather hot bidding going on our first item, an important Italian piano once owned by Thelonious Monk."

The auctioneer gestured to his right, where three men were busy rolling the piano up a ramp and onto the platform. Another man followed them, carrying the matching high-back bench. Once the piano and bench were in place on the platform, the workers left and the auctioneer began speaking again.

"There was a call-in bid of forty thousand dollars during the last auction. That would have been the winning bid, but we were unable to reach the bidder for verification. Therefore we will start tonight's bidding at our last verified price, thirty thousand dollars."

Lina raised her paddle without hesitation. Unfortunately, so did six other people in the room, including Mrs. Parker and Rashad.

The auctioneer continued. "Do I hear thirty-five? I have thirty-five. Who'll give me forty…?"

As the amount of the bid increased, Lina kept raising her paddle. She knew her upper limit was sixty thousand dollars, and she'd hoped the bids would stay well south of that. Now it was obvious that wasn't going to be the case. Doing her best to keep her nerves from getting the best of her, she kept up with the bidding, being sure to observe those around her.

By the time the bid reached fifty-five thousand, only three paddles remained raised. Lina held hers up, as did Mrs. Parker and Rashad. She could feel the perspiration dampening her hairline. Neither of them seemed willing to back down.

"Who'll give me sixty thousand?"

Mrs. Parker sighed, shook her head and dropped her paddle. "It isn't worth that much to me."

Lina's head swiveled, her gaze connecting with Rashad. It was down to just the two of them now. Sixty thousand dollars was a lot of money, and frankly more than she wanted to spend. She couldn't go any higher, but as she stared at him, she prayed he couldn't read the nervousness on her face.

The auctioneer looked at the two of them. "Will one of you give me sixty-five?"

"I will." The words escaped Lina's mouth before common sense could halt them. Where she would get another five grand, she didn't know. Nevertheless, she would figure it out. A smile curved her lips when she saw Rashad's blank expression. Was he finally conceding defeat?

Then his expression changed.

He placed his paddle on the seat next to him, and stood.

Lina folded her arms, prepared to watch him walk out.

The auctioneer's voice boomed in the near silence. "Sixty-five thousand going once…"

Rashad straightened his jacket, adjusted his tie.

"Going twice…"

Lina clutched her purse to her chest. *I'm about to win!*

Just as the auctioneer opened his mouth again, Rashad cut him off.

In a clear, confident voice, he announced a bid. "One hundred thousand dollars."

A gasp escaped Lina, her mouth dropping open. Where in the hell was Rashad getting that kind of money? Were his parents financing this? She knew their company was successful, but this was far beyond what she could have imagined.

The auctioneer's broad grin belied his excitement. "Going once, going twice, sold to the gentleman in blue for one hundred thousand dollars."

Her hands still clenched around the purse, Lina got to her feet. Shock and hurt filled her, and even though she was only feet away from Rashad, she noted that he was going out of his way to avoid making eye contact with her.

Tears filled her eyes. After everything they'd shared, everything he'd meant to her, she'd thought things were different. Now she understood why he'd seemed so aloof about the auction, he'd known all along he had the resources to win. He'd been playing her all this time.

In the short time since Monk's piano had brought them together again, he'd won her heart. She knew she was in love with him, but now she realized he couldn't be trusted. If he could hide something like this from her, who knew what other secrets he might keep?

With tears rolling down her cheeks, she stepped away from her seat and marched down the center aisle.

She could hear Rashad's voice calling her name, but she didn't stop or look back.


The bright, sun-drenched Saturday morning sent light streaming through the picture window into Rashad's den. As he stood there, staring at the spot he'd just cleared and vacuumed for Monk's piano, he sighed. Despite the boon of winning the bid, and being only hours away from taking delivery on a priceless piece of musical history, his mood was as foul as the weather was beautiful.

He walked across the room, his bare feet sinking into the plush, cream-colored carpeting. With his back against the wall, he took a seat on the floor. Occupying the spot that would soon be taken up by the piano, and dropped his head into his hands. He'd initially gone to Cleveland and Wendell with his heart set on winning the piano. Running into Lina had been a happy coincidence. Now that it was over, he couldn't believe the way things had turned out. He never would have thought winning would leave him feeling such a deep sense of loss.

"You're a pitiful sight, do you know that?"

He dropped his hands and looked up at the sound of his sister's voice. "Simone, not right now."

Simone, still in her aquarium-themed pajama pants

and T-shirt, strode over and sat on the floor directly in front of him. "Just stating the facts, bro."

He groaned. "Why are you torturing me? It's bad enough I've lost Lina."

She shrugged her shoulders. "Well, I'm not one to say I told you so, but..."

He rolled his eyes. "Please. You *are* one to say it, and you enjoy it."

"Anyway, the brother I know would not be sitting here moping. He would be going after his woman."

He let his head drop back against the wall. "I don't think she wants to talk to me, Simone. I tried talking to her after I won the bid, and she ignored me. I've been blowing up her phone, but she won't take my calls."

"Have you gone to her house?"

"You mean, so she can slam the door in my face? No, I haven't."

Simone rose to her feet, shaking her head. "I know you're not going to let the possibility of having a door slammed in your face stop you from trying. I used to slam the door on you all the time, and it never kept you from getting all up in my grill."

He felt a smile tug at his lips, despite his mood. Simone had always been a pistol, and at every attempt he'd made to protect her, she'd gotten mad and claimed he was in her business. She was right, though, he had to at least give it a shot. He braced himself and climbed up from his spot on the floor.

She smiled. "There you go, bro."

"I'm going over there. But look, the delivery men

will be here soon with the piano. Can you make sure they get it in here without damaging it?"

Simone raised her hand to her forehead in mock salute. "It shall be done, sir."

Chuckling at his sister's weird sense of humor, he turned and went to his bedroom to get quickly dressed.

Within the hour, he pulled his truck into Lina's driveway. Her car was parked there, so he assumed she was at home. In any other case he would have called ahead, but since she'd been screening his calls, there really wasn't any point in doing that.

He climbed down from his truck, flowers in hand, and shut the door behind him. He strode up the walk and stepped onto her porch. Taking a deep breath, he raised his fist to knock on the door.

She swung it open before he could.

Her face, despite her annoyed expression, was still as beautiful as a sunrise on the ocean. She wore a long cotton nightgown, pink with little white ribbons at the front. It was far more matronly than anything he thought she'd own, but he could clearly recall the feminine curves hidden beneath it. Her hair was brushed behind her ears.

Opening her pursed lips, she asked, "Rashad, what the hell are you doing here?"

He extended the bouquet of yellow roses and larkspur in her direction. "I just wanted to talk to you, but you're not taking my calls."

She folded her arms over her chest. "And you didn't take that as a hint that I didn't want to be bothered with you?"

Noticing she didn't seem interested in the flowers, he set them down on the windowsill next to the door. "Look, I'm sorry about this whole thing with the piano. The men are delivering it today, and if you really want it, I'm happy to give it to you."

She rolled her eyes so hard he'd swear she could see the future. "Seriously, Rashad? You really think this is about the piano?"

Confusion knit his brow, and he shifted his weight to lean against the brick wall beside the door. "Then what is it about?"

Standing in the doorway, she shook her head. "You still don't get it, Rashad. Did you think I wouldn't notice that bid? Did you really think I wouldn't be curious to know where you got a hundred grand from, when you just lost your job?"

His eyes slid closed. It was happening, just the way Simone had forewarned. *Damn, I hate when she's right.* "Lina, baby, listen—"

"No, you listen. What kind of shit are you involved in? For all I know you could be running drugs from South America. Or did your mommy and daddy front you the money? Either way, you've been keeping something from me, and you know I demand honesty."

His brow hitched up, as a mixture of humor and disbelief coursed through him. "Running drugs from South America? You've got one hell of an imagination."

Apparently she didn't see anything funny, because her expression remained just as stormy. "Six years ago, I would have thought it was far-fetched to think my ex-husband would be unfaithful. I thought my friends were making up stories when they tried to tell me about his near-constant cheating. He lied to my face, repeatedly. Thought I was too stupid to figure it out, or too weak to call him on it. So don't stand here making jokes about my 'wild imagination,' Rashad. Don't insult me."

He straightened, feeling properly chastised. "I'm sorry, Lina. I didn't mean it like that. But you have to hear me out."

"Honesty, Rashad. That's all I asked of you, and you refused to give it."

He could see her anger fading as it morphed into sadness. "Baby, I swear, I can explain everything."

The tears gathered in her eyes, and she dashed away one that spilled down her cheek. "You had plenty of time to tell me before, Rashad. Whatever it is, I don't want to hear it. And I don't want to see you again, ever." She stepped back.

"Lina, wait. Don't…"

Before he could finish his sentence, she'd retreated inside and slammed the door. Now he heard the lock turn, and her footfalls as she walked away, retreating farther into the house.

He stood there on her porch for a few silent minutes, taking in the finality of her words. Tightness rose in his chest, and he felt as if his heart were being wrenched in a vise.

He hadn't told her the whole truth, and now she hated him. Regardless of how over the top he'd thought her trust issues were, she had a right to guard her own heart in any way she saw fit. He'd brought this on himself, and now he'd have to pay for his stubbornness. The punishment of a life spent without her seemed too much to bear, but he couldn't think of anything else he could say or do that would make her change her mind.

In stoic silence, he turned and walked back to his truck.

## Chapter 15

Lina let her eyes close, and enjoyed the feeling of coolness as the esthetician placed the fresh cucumber slices on her eyelids. Her face already tingled from the tea tree and vitamin E mask she'd been wearing for the past twenty minutes, and as the stack of heated blankets were placed over her robe-clad body, she sank into the padded table.

She was just beginning to enjoy her warm cocoon of luxury when her mother's voice cut into her reverie.

"Lina, you know I'm not one to get in your business."

Beneath the cucumbers, she rolled her eyes. She knew her mother couldn't detect her movement, since they were lying next to each other on tables in Serenity

Spa, each similarly covered in blankets and face gunk. "Mama, please don't. I'm trying to relax."

Carla sighed. "I know that, but it's not my fault you can't relax. You're feeling emotional, and we both know why."

Lina groaned under her breath. Regardless of the way she felt, she knew better than to disrespect her mother. Grown or not, she knew Carla Smith would give her a fat lip if she did. "Mama, you know I love you, but I really don't want to talk about this right now."

"Well, that's tough. You're not going to ruin my day at the spa with that salty attitude, missy. So we're going to talk about it."

She could tell from her mother's tone that she intended to hash this thing out, whether Lina liked it or not. Settling into the padded table, she acquiesced. "Okay, Mama. What do you have to say?"

"Nothing, yet. I want to hear what you have to say."

Lina blew out a breath. A moment ago, she'd thought listening to her mother lecture her would be the worst of it. But this, being forced to relive it all and dredge up all the bad emotions swirling around inside of her, was bound to be far more unpleasant. "I already told you, Mama. He's still lying to me after everything we've been through together, and you know I can't stand being lied to."

"So you're going to tell me that you're not mad he won that piano that you wanted to give me?"

She removed the cucumbers, and opened her eyes. When she turned her head toward her mother, she found her already watching her. "Of course I'm upset about that. I really wanted you to have that piano, because I know how much you love Monk's music."

Her mama's face, painted blue with the anti-aging algae mask she wore, twisted into a frown. "Girl, did you ever stop and think if I wanted the piano? Or where I would put it? That thing was about the size of a small barge."

Her brow furrowed. "You mean you wouldn't have wanted it?"

"I didn't say that. It's just that you didn't ask me. I know you wanted to surprise me, but for someone like me, living in a two-bedroom house, owning something like that would just be silly and impractical."

"If I'd won the bid, what would you have done with the piano?"

Her mother looked thoughtful for a minute. "Seems to me, something like that belongs in a museum. Monk was born here in North Carolina, up in Rocky Mount. Maybe they'd want it up there, to put on display."

In that moment, Lina realized that she'd been so determined to get the piano, she hadn't really given much thought to what her mother would do with it. "I see your point, but it's just like I told him. The piano isn't the issue here, dishonesty is."

"Mmm-hmm." It was the telltale sound of skepticism.

Lina lifted her head and shoulders off the table to look at her mother. "What? I'm serious. He's obviously doing something on the side, if he can still have all this money after losing his job at the courthouse. And his bid was extravagant, way beyond what he needed to spend to win. It's like he was showing off."

"How do you know he's doing something on the side? What if he spent his life savings on the piano? He's a grown man, and whether you like it or not he can spend *his* money as *he* sees fit."

She held back the eye roll she felt coming on, since they were both without their cucumber slices. "Something just doesn't feel right. Didn't you teach me to go with my gut?"

"Is your gut really telling you he's doing something wrong? Or are you just mad that you don't know his whole life story?"

Lina started to launch a retort, but quieted. She'd spent the past two nights making all kinds of assumptions about what Rashad might be doing to have access to that kind of money. When he'd stood on her porch the previous morning, looking and smelling as delicious as a five-layer chocolate cake, he'd probably been trying to explain his financial situation, but she'd been so angry and hurt she didn't let him finish. While the pain still remained, her anger had tapered off significantly, and if she were honest with herself, she'd have to admit that she missed him. There was no way she was going to admit that to her mother, though.

Carla shook her head. "Ever since you found out what an ass Warren was and divorced him, you've been holding on to this grudge against men. I haven't liked none of the idiots you've dated, but I like Rashad. He's a good man, Lina. I'm telling you, if you don't come to your senses and stop all this bitterness, you're going to regret it."

Tears started to gather in Lina's eyes, and she held them back as best she could. There just wasn't any good way to wipe your face when it was smeared with tea tree mask. "Mama, I don't want to get hurt again. I don't think I can take another heartbreak."

"I know, baby. I know. I don't want to see you hurt again, either. But I honestly don't believe Rashad is out to hurt you."

Lina sniffled, dabbed at her eyes with the corner of one of the blankets heaped atop her.

"You don't have to go after him. If I'm right, and I usually am, he'll be back to make his case again. All I'm asking of you is to give the man a fair shot at explaining himself. If you don't like what you hear then, I'll let it go. Okay?"

She looked into her mother's loving eyes, and nodded. "Fair enough, Mama."

"Good." She lay back again and put the cucumbers back over her eyes. "Now you can relax."

Shaking her head, Lina replaced her own cucumber slices and lay back on the table. Her mother had given her plenty to think about. Her mind fixated on Rashad, and she replayed the vivid memories of his kiss, his touch and his expert lovemaking. The warmth of ten heated blankets was lovely, but it wasn't nearly as wonderful as the feel of his hard, naked body cradling against hers. In his arms, she'd found true passion, and his touch had been the antidote to her stressful days at work. Now that she'd experienced his loving, her life would never be the same. She doubted very seriously that any other man could compete with the erotic memories he'd left her with. Could she really go the rest of her life without the thrill of everything he'd given her?

The soft music and the lure of the warm blankets got the better of her, and soon, she drifted off to sleep.

And while she napped, those passion filled memories of Rashad and his lovemaking haunted her dreams.

Rashad reached behind him to wrap an elastic band around his locks, to keep them out of his face. He eased onto the bench and flexed his hands over the keyboard, stretching his joints. He was at Marco's house for Monday night rehearsal, and he expected to play and sing pretty hard today. At a time like this, when emotion threatened to rise to the surface, he escaped into the comfort of music.

Around him, the others were busy setting up to play, as well. Ken was already stationed behind the drum set. Marco adjusted the strap holding his tenor saxophone around his neck and Darius plucked a few notes on Miss Molly, his beloved upright bass.

Marco, his strap now adjusted to his liking, clapped his hands together. "All right. Rashad, you're picking the set for this week. What do you have?"

Rashad reached into his pocket and pulled out the list of songs he'd chosen. Unfolding the paper, he handed it to Marco.

Marco's brow furrowed as he read the song titles aloud. "'Hard Hearted Hannah,' 'I Got It Bad and That

Ain't Good,' 'Stormy Weather'… Jeez, Rashad, is it that bad, man?"

Rashad looked up from the keyboard to see everyone in the room staring at him. "What? We can't just be singing the same love songs all the time. Love is complicated, and sometimes it goes wrong."

Ken, tapping out a slow rhythm on the snare, quipped, "Yeah, but based on that set list, love didn't just go bad, it died a slow and painful death."

Darius chuckled, with a shake of his head. "Seriously, Rashad. This is a concert, not a funeral."

Rashad folded his arms over his chest. Sounding much angrier than he intended, he growled, "Ha-ha. Y'all are so damn funny. Regardless, it was my turn to pick the set list, so deal with it."

Ken laid down his sticks and put his hands up in a gesture of surrender. "Whatever, man. Just chill."

Leaning his bass against the wall, Darius cocked his head to the side. "Nah, man. You can't be expecting us to play all this sad music just because you're in a funk. The female fans expect better from us."

Rashad got to his feet, hands balled into fists. "Don't press me on this, D."

Darius looked him dead in the eye. "If you wanna square up, go ahead. But you know good and damn well that I'm right."

Marco, finding himself standing between the two of them, took a big step back. Ken, eyes wide, stayed behind the drum set, and remained quiet.

Tension crackled in the room like static electricity as Rashad and Darius stared each other down.

Anger coursed through Rashad like hot lava, but as he looked at Darius, the best friend he'd ever had, he knew his anger was misdirected. They'd tussled before, but not since college. He knew Darius could hold his own in a fight. And when it came down to brass tacks, there was no reason for them to be fighting.

Rashad took a deep breath, relaxed his hands at his sides. "You're right, man. I'm sorry."

Darius relaxed as well, and the tension seemed to drain from the atmosphere. "I'm glad you see my point. I don't mind a few of these brokenhearted songs, let's just mix it up with something more upbeat, okay?"

Rashad nodded as he went back to his seat behind the keyboard. "I'm good with that. Y'all pick three songs, and we'll mix those with my first three. Deal?"

Everyone seemed agreeable, so they drafted a new set list, then shuffled through their sheet music collection for the songs they didn't know by heart.

Marco snapped his fingers, as if he'd just remembered something. "I forgot to tell you. Rudy over at the Blue Lounge called me. He says that piano they ordered for the club came in today."

Clapping his hands together, Rashad perked up. "Great. It's an upright, I'm guessing?"

Marco wet his reed, placed it in the slot at the mouthpiece of his sax. "Yeah, Rudy says they couldn't fit a baby grand since the stage is so small. It's supposed to be a top-of-the-line model, though."

Rashad was glad to hear that the piano had finally come in. He didn't mind playing the keyboard per se, but to his mind, nothing matched the clear, pure sound of an actual piano. He'd offered to bring in the one he had at home, but Rudy, the owner of the Blue, had told him there wasn't room for a piano that size. Rashad hadn't played an upright since his college days, but it would still be a marked improvement from playing a keyboard during shows.

Darius called out to him, breaking through his thoughts. "Rashad, are you gonna be all right, man?"

Rashad looked over at his friend, and saw the genuine concern in his eyes. "Yeah, D. I'll be all right."

Darius responded with a grin and a wink.

Rashad smiled. He remembered the crestfallen look on Darius's face all those months ago, when Darius was sure he'd lost his chance at being with Eve. They'd gotten through it, and now were married, expecting and deliriously happy. That thought gave him hope that he might somehow mend his broken relationship with Lina.

Taking a deep breath, he set his focus on Ken, who counted off the start of the first song.

Rashad put his fingers to the keys, and once cued, sang and played as passionately as his feelings for Lina demanded.

## Chapter 16

Tuesday evening, Lina sat in the passenger seat of Tara Mitchell's midsize sedan, watching the scenery of the Queen City roll by. When Tara had entered her office an hour ago and offered her a ride to the Park Hotel, she'd accepted. The firm often used the meeting rooms at the Park when they had to schmooze wealthy clients. Lina assumed that to be the reason Gwendolyn had asked the entire staff to meet her there at six thirty that evening.

Her eyes on the road, Tara mused out loud. "I wonder who the client is this time."

Lina shrugged. "I don't know. I asked Gwen earlier, but she's being pretty tight-lipped about this one. Must be somebody famous."

"Ooh, what if it's J. Cole. He's from Fayetteville, you know. Girl, if it is, I'll die!"

Tara spent the rest of the ride hypothesizing aloud on who the client might be. Lina, while curious, just didn't have the brain space to dedicate to a guessing game. All she could think about was Rashad, and how badly she missed him. She couldn't bring herself to call, though she knew he'd take her call. She was so torn about the whole situation, her emotions wouldn't allow her to pick up the phone. But she still held out some hope that he'd contact her. It had only been three days since she'd slammed the door in his face.

When Tara pulled her car into a parking space at the Park Hotel, she and Lina climbed out with briefcases and handbags in tow. They entered the lobby, greeting the front desk staff as they made their way to the Maple suite, the room the firm had always used when at the hotel.

The lights seemed a bit dim to Lina as they moved down the corridor, but she didn't pay it much attention. She and Tara were still chatting when she swung open the double doors to the room.

*"Surprise!"*

Lina dropped her purse as she looked around the room at all her coworkers from the firm. The Maple suite had been draped in black and silver finery, and a large sign hanging across the front wall read Congratulations Lina and Tara.

Tara's hand flew to her mouth. "You guys!"

Lina, still in shock, felt a smile spreading across her face. "Wow." As she looked around, she spotted her mother as well as Eve and Darius among the smiling faces present in the room. She also saw Barton, Tara's longtime boyfriend, standing amid the partygoers. Obviously, someone had put a great deal of effort into planning this little soiree. Despite her pain over Rashad, she couldn't help but be touched by the kind gesture.

Gwendolyn stepped out of the crowd, a broad smile on her face. "Welcome, ladies. I just want to say congratulations, and that I'm so glad to have you two as my newest senior partners."

Applause and cheers filled the room.

Waiters fanned out through the space, passing around filled flutes of champagne. As Lina accepted her glass, she offered a smile to her mother, who blew her a kiss in response.

Once everyone had been served, Gwendolyn raised her glass. "A toast to the women of the hour, Lina and Tara."

"Hear, hear."

The collective sound of glasses clinking together soon gave way to the din of many competing conversations.

Lina hugged Tara and Gwendolyn, then walked over to where her mother stood with Darius and Eve. "How long have you all been keeping this secret from me?"

Eve chuckled. "Gwen called us a couple of weeks ago about it."

Playfully, Lina punched Eve in the shoulder. "I can't believe you held it in that long."

"That's why I've been keeping her so busy at home,

so she wouldn't have the time or the strength to spill the beans." Darius drew his wife close to his side and gave her a soft kiss on the lips.

Watching them sent a twinge through her, as she remembered the way Rashad kissed her.

Carla grabbed her, pulling her into an embrace. "Oh, I'm so proud of you, baby!"

She could hear the emotion in her mother's voice. "Thanks, Mama. Come on now, don't cry."

Dashing away a few tears, Carla smiled. "I'll be all right. That's just the pride leaking out through my eyes, that's all."

Laughing at her mother's turn of phrase, she kissed her on the cheek. "I love you, too, Mama."

Lina moved around the room, stopping to speak to her coworkers, and to Barton, who had his arm draped around Tara. When she'd finished making her rounds, she took a seat near the rear of the room, beneath the banner. There, a large window looked out on a courtyard behind the hotel. The scenery was beautiful. There was a large three-tiered fountain, with crystal clear water cascading down toward the small pool at the bottom. Surrounding the fountains were hundreds of brightly colored blooms, including raspberry-pink petunias, sunny-yellow impatiens and snowy white phlox. Gazing at the cascading water and the colorful flowers, she felt some of the tension inside of her draining away.

Behind her, the conversation suddenly halted. Wondering what had made everybody go silent, she swiveled in her seat to see.

There, standing in the open doors of the room, was Rashad.

He wore a royal blue suit, black shirt and royal blue tie. His locks were left free, the brown tips hanging around his shoulders. In his arms, he carried what had to be the biggest bouquet of roses, larkspur and lamb's ears she'd ever seen.

His eyes were fixed on her as he started to walk in her direction.

She got to her feet, wanting to meet him halfway. She was so mesmerized by the sight of him, however, that she couldn't get her feet moving.

So she just stood there in silence, like everyone else in the room, and watched him walk. God, how she loved to watch him walk.

When he reached her, he handed over the humongous bouquet. She set it on the chair she'd just vacated.

Their eyes locked.

The open palms of his big hands rose to gently grasp her bare forearms. His sexy, full lips parted. "Lina, I have a trust fund. I should have told you about it from the beginning, but I haven't had positive experiences with women who knew about it in the past. I should have known you weren't like them, and I should have been honest with you. I'm sorry, baby. Please forgive me."

She looked up at him, felt her body moving closer to his of its own accord. When she was chest to chest with him, she wrapped her arms around his neck. The words in her heart tumbled from her mouth on a breathless sigh. "I forgive you."

A smile spread across his handsome face. "That's the best thing I've heard all day."

Cheers and applause erupted as he leaned down and touched his lips to hers. Everybody in the room was now privy to her personal business, but as her lips parted and his tongue darted inside her mouth, she didn't care. His kiss sent shock waves of desire radiating through her whole body.

When he finally broke the kiss, she wove her hands into the dark riches of his hair. "I'm glad you came here, Rashad."

His eyes smoldering with heat, he stroked a fingertip along her cheek. "I wouldn't miss this for anything in the world."

A sigh escaped her, and as he dipped his head to kiss her again, she melted into his embrace.

Doing his best to keep his focus on the road and off his incredibly sexy passenger, Rashad drove his truck through the streets of downtown Charlotte. They'd tucked her flowers, along with her briefcase and blazer, into the back of the extended cab and hit the road only a few minutes ago. As he pulled up to a red light, he took the opportunity to let his eyes feast on the beauty of his queen.

Lina wore a black pencil skirt and a sleeveless white button-down blouse. A string of pearls around her neck matched the small studs in her ears, and her hair was in its naturally curly state, held back from her face by a glittery white headband. A pair of black peep toe pumps capped her long legs. The outfit was simple and professional, but on her, drop-dead sexy.

"So, you're not going to tell me where we're going?" She gazed out the window as she posed the question, as if she could use the passing scenery to discern their destination.

He shook his head. "Nope. I told you, it's a surprise."

"Come on, I've already been surprised once today. Besides, there's nowhere I want to go right now other than your place. We're due for some serious makeup sex, boo."

A tremble of desire ran through him, and his body responded to the sensual invitation in her voice. "Trust and believe, baby, I'm gonna give you what you're asking for before the night is out. We just have to make a stop first."

She offered him a mock pout, which soon dissolved into a smile.

He felt his own grin broaden in response. Yesterday he'd been worried he'd never be blessed with her smile again. Now he wanted to spend the rest of his life keeping that gorgeous smile on her face.

Reaching the parking lot of the Afro-American Arts Museum, he pulled the truck into a space. He cut the engine and hopped out, tucked his keys into his pocket. After walking to the passenger side, he opened the door and helped her down.

The question he sensed she would ask was out of her mouth before her foot left the running board. "What are we doing here?"

Seeing her safely to the ground, he held fast to her soft-skinned hand. "You'll see in a minute. Come on."

He hit the button on his keys to lock the truck while he led her through the glass doors and into the museum's lobby. Inside, he nodded to the staff member posted behind the desk. After they exchanged a few words, Rashad led her down a corridor to the main exhibition hall.

"I haven't been here in a couple of years," she commented. "My father used to volunteer here, though. He loved this place."

Once they were inside the large marble floored room, Lina looked around for a few minutes, taking in the artifacts displayed there. He knew when she finally saw it, because she gasped.

"Oh my God." She clasped a hand over her mouth.

There, in the center of the room, sat Monk's spectacular gilded piano, along with the matching bench. The museum staff had cordoned it off with a set of burgundy velvet ropes, and a sign with the words Please Do Not Touch rested atop the piano's hood.

She let go of his hand, walked closer to the piano. "It really is a work of art. It belongs here, doesn't it?"

Rashad nodded. "Yes. It was pretty selfish of me to want to keep it to myself. Now everyone can enjoy it, including your mother."

She rested her palm on one of the rope stands, shaking her head. "To think we spent all that time fussing about it, now neither of us has it."

"I'll get to see it as often as I like, since I'm going to be working here as a curator."

She turned toward him, her expression somewhat confused. "Really? Even with the trust fund, you still want to work?"

He shrugged. "I worked at the courthouse all those years, why not? I know I'll actually enjoy working here and, besides, work ethic is part of who I am."

She nodded, seemingly impressed. "Okay, then. Thanks for bringing me here to see it."

"No problem. Now, about that makeup sex…"

She walked back over to him, raised up on her toes to kiss him on the cheek. "Let's go."

They were back outside and in his truck within a couple of minutes.

As he guided the truck out of the lot and into traffic, he knew it was time to tell her the full story. "My family's furniture company is very successful, and if I wanted to, I could step into an executive position at any time. I moved here to Charlotte to start my own life, away from the family business."

She nodded, but asked, "Why? Why would you want to escape what could have been an easy life?"

He sighed. "My grandfather, Solomon. He founded MacRae Incorporated back in the fifties. I remember him as a cruel, mean-spirited man who lorded his wealth and power over others, and I vowed never to be like him. To me, that meant leaving the family business behind."

She was quiet for a few moments, as if mulling over what he said. "Do you know what made him that way?"

He nodded as he turned the wheel, directing the truck into his subdivision. "Yes. My parents told me about it. My grandfather married my grandmother after the company started to take off, and apparently he loved her fiercely. She didn't share his feelings, though, having married him just for the lifestyle he could provide her. She carried on affairs through their entire marriage, and when he finally confronted her, she demanded a divorce."

"Wow."

"Wow is right. After my grandmother walked out of his life, he became embittered, taking out his pain on everyone else. He never remarried, and never recovered from her betrayal."

She whistled. "Now I see why you didn't tell me about your finances. It must have been hard growing up with someone like that in your life."

He had to agree with her assessment. "I guess that plays into why I didn't want you to know about my trust fund. I wanted to be sure you loved me for who I was, not for what I could give you."

She reached out, laying her hand on his thigh. The heat of her touch seemed to singe his skin through the fabric of his slacks. "I do love you, Rashad. I honestly, truly do."

He squeezed her hand as he pulled into his driveway. "I know you do, baby. And I love you." He hit the button on the remote attached to his headliner, opening the garage door.

Once the truck was parked and the door lowered, he went around to her side. Opening the door he scooped her out, draping her body over his shoulder.

"Rashad!" His name escaped her lips on a squeal of delight.

With one hand firmly planted on her ass, he fished his keys from the pocket of his slacks, unlocked the side door and carried her into the house. She giggled all the way to his bedroom, where he gently lay her body across his king-size bed.

He wanted more than anything to kiss her, to let his tongue and his hands become thoroughly reacquainted with the tastes and feel of her. He held his raging desire in check in favor of taking his time. Because tonight, it wasn't just about makeup sex. No, this was a celebration of their love and new commitment to each other, and he planned to give it to her until she sang his name. He never wanted her to forget this night.

So while she lay sprawled across his bed, watching him, he finished the preparations he'd begun earlier in the day in hopes she'd forgive him. He got the long-nosed candle lighter from his nightstand drawer and moved around the room lighting the candles he'd already put in place. Then he grabbed the remote to his stereo system and pressed Play. The playlist he'd queued up earlier began to play, starting with Raheem Devaughn's recent album.

As the thumping beat of the second track began, she sat up in bed. "So it's like that?"

Shrugging out of his sport coat, he held her gaze. "Oh, yeah, baby. It's like that."

# Chapter 17

With appreciative eyes, Lina watched Rashad strip away his clothes, one item at a time. First his sport coat hit the floor, then his tie. His big hands unfastened the buttons running down the front of his shirt, and his eyes met hers as he tossed the shirt and the tank beneath it away.

Lina sucked in a breath through clenched teeth as she was met with the sight of the rippling muscles of his upper body. His hands went to the front of his slacks, and he unbuttoned them, letting them slide down his powerful thighs.

At this point she realized she'd slid to the edge of the bed. She started undoing the buttons of her blouse, only to have him gesture for her to stop.

"No, baby. I'll handle that."

Obediently she dropped her hands to her sides.

Wearing nothing but his blue silk boxers, he strode over to the bed. Weaving his hands into her hair, he leaned down to kiss her lips. Then his magical mouth moved to her neck, his tongue darting out of his mouth to graze over the sensitive skin. His hands undid her buttons and slipped the blouse down her arms and off her body. He backed off a bit, smiling at the sight of her black lace bra.

Her head fell back as he planted a kiss above the tiny bow centering the cups of the bra, and reached around her to undo the clasp. Several heated moments passed as he undressed her, pausing to kiss and caress each area of flesh he unveiled. Her body obeyed his every unspoken command. Though she was barely aware of it as her hips rose from the bed so he could do away with her skirt and panties.

He stood before her as if admiring her nudity. "You're so, so beautiful."

"So are you…" The words slipped from her lips as her hand trailed up his hard thigh. She found the slit in the front of his boxers, and eased her hand inside.

"Lina." He breathily husked out her name as she freed his hardness from between the open halves of the fabric.

She said nothing, leaning forward to capture him in her mouth.

His hands first landed on her shoulders, then moved up when he threaded his fingers through her hair. She could feel the subtle movement of his hips as she loved him the same way he'd loved her, attentively and with ardor. To increase his pleasure, she hummed along with the familiar track playing in the background, while he was still in her mouth.

"Ah." He groaned, drew her away.

Looking up at him, she winked.

"Woman, you are wicked."

She offered him a bedroom-eyed smile. "Only for you."

With a growl, he leaned down to kiss her again. As the kiss deepened, they moved in tandem toward the center of the mattress. Fluidly, she moved so that he was on his back, and before he could take over again, she straddled him.

He reached beneath the pillow, extracting a condom, and handed it to her.

"You must have been pretty sure I'd forgive you."

He gave her bottom a firm smack. "What can I say, I'm an optimistic man."

Shaking her head, she unwrapped the condom. They maneuvered a bit so he could remove his boxers, and she covered his hardness. She tossed the pack away, then centered her body over his.

His open palms caressing her hips, she lowered herself onto him. Both of them sighed as their bodies joined, and she could feel the hot liquid desire he'd built in her enveloping him. Once she'd taken him in as deeply as she could, she shuddered and, lifting her hips, she began to ride.

She watched his face, and saw his eyes roll up into his head as she fell into a rhythm that matched the slow, sexy beat of the music. His big hands palmed her ass, and she could hear his low growl mixing with the sounds of her own moans. He filled her so well, touching places inside her that set her very soul aflame. Before she knew it, she could feel the opening notes of orgasm building within.

He grasped her hips firmly, halting her motion. "I'm taking over, baby."

She could do nothing more than grab his shoulders and hold on as his hips began to piston upward, driving his hardness in and out of her body. She felt the blissful friction increasing in tandem with his powerful upward thrusts as he drove her closer and closer to madness. She moaned, sighed and finally cried out as the building pleasure reached its peak. She flung her head back and sang his name on the wings of ecstasy and, soon after, heard him roar as he found his own release.

She came back to herself then, moving around until she lay flat on top of him, her head resting against his chest. The cadence of his beating heart was just as rapid as her own. He draped his strong arms around her, and she relished the feel of being held by the man she loved.

She gave his sweat-dampened chest an affectionate stroke. "Are you awake?"

His husky reply filled the silence. "Yeah."

"I know I told you I forgive you, and I do."

He kissed the top of her head. "Thank you for forgiving me, baby."

Tucking one arm beneath him, she cuddled closer to the warm lines of his hard body. "I'm just glad you finally opened up to me. That was all I ever really wanted, to know you fully." She had to admit she was curious about the details of his trust fund, but she didn't ask. When he felt comfortable enough, she was sure he'd tell her.

"From now on, there will be no more secrets between us. I promise."

She could feel the smile lifting the corners of her mouth, because deep down, she trusted him to keep his word. "There is something else that I need to say, and it's important."

He tensed a bit beneath her. "What is it?"

She sighed. "I love you, Rashad. And you may as well know, since there's no way I can deny it now."

He shifted, used his hand to cup her chin. Tilting her face up, he gazed into her eyes. "I love you, Lina."

She touched her lips to his, and as the kiss deepened she realized that she'd never felt safer or more at peace than she did lying in his arms.

Balancing an aluminum pan filled with grilled meat, Rashad maneuvered around the gaggle of folks standing on the patio and set the pan down on the table. The Emerald Isle beach house, owned by Darius and Eve, was crawling with people who'd come together for a nontraditional baby shower of sorts for the couple. Eve, now in her second trimester, had insisted on having a cookout and inviting all their good friends, instead of the traditional female-only affair.

The house was located on a wide band of private beach, accessed by a flight of stairs descending from the glazed oak patio. Down there, a volleyball net had been anchored in the white sand, and several people were participating in a match. Opened beach umbrellas dotted the landscape, and beyond the strip of sand lay the endless, rippling blue-gray waters of the Atlantic.

As Rashad moved back to his post by the grill, he elbowed Darius, who was busy brushing sauce onto several racks of baby back ribs. "Dude, I thought I was an invited guest here. Why do you have me working the grill with you?"

Darius grinned. "C'mon, Rashad. You're no guest. You're family."

"And that means putting me to work?"

"Damn skippy." Darius gave him a playful punch in the shoulder.

He rolled his eyes. It had been a good hour or more since he'd seen Lina, and he was starting to get antsy. Generally he didn't mind helping out with something like this, but he knew he'd enjoy the task all the more if he had his sweetheart nearby.

As if on cue, Lina walked up the patio stairs.

Again, Rashad took in the sight of her. She was wearing a white halter top and a bright orange maxi skirt dotted with white flowers. Her hair was held back from her face by a glittery elastic band, and as she lifted her skirt and stepped onto the patio, he could see that she'd kicked off her sandals.

When their eyes met, she smiled, and he felt the fluttering in his heart. He wanted to spend the rest of his days bringing her the same joy she brought him.

She made her way through the people hanging out on the patio and entered his personal space.

She inhaled deeply. "Smells good up here, boys. Any idea when the food will be ready?"

"Twenty minutes or so, then we can eat," Darius answered.

She nodded, but never tore her eyes away from him. "Rashad, are you gonna be released from grill duty anytime soon?"

He looped his arms around her waist, pulled her body close to his. "Why? Do you miss me, baby?"

A wicked smile crossed her face. She leaned up to kiss him on the cheek, then whispered in his ear. "You know I do, after the way you had me screaming your name last night."

He dropped one of his hands lower to give her ass a firm squeeze.

Darius cleared his throat. "Y'all cut that out before you burn my chicken, man."

With a chuckle, Rashad acquiesced. Giving his beautiful queen a quick peck on the lips and a smack on the bottom, he sent her back down to the beach.

"It's good to see you and Lina back on good terms." Darius grabbed a pair of tongs and adjusted the position of his ribs on the grate.

"We're on fantastic terms." His eyes followed Lina as she walked down the beach toward Eve and some of the other women gathered around a small fire pit. The seductive sway of her hips made him want to eschew his duties and the gathering so he could spirit her away to someplace private. When he turned back toward the grill, he felt his friend's eyes on him. "What?"

Darius folded his arms over his chest. "I know the feeling, and I know that look in your eyes. When are you going to pop the big question, man?"

Rashad shrugged, closing the grill lid so the last few chicken wings could finish cooking through. "Soon, I guess. I'm waiting for just the right moment."

"Whatever. If you know like I know, you'd better make it official ASAP. Don't give her any reason to doubt your commitment."

He could tell Darius was looking past him, probably at Eve. "I guess you're the expert now, since you're married, and about to be a father."

"I'm no expert, but I know what I know. The love of a good woman is the best thing that can happen to a man." Swiping his hands on a towel hanging from the grill handle, he smiled. "Do you think I'll do all right at this fatherhood thing?"

Rashad made a show of thinking about it. "I guess so. I mean, you've done a good job of ordering us around in the past, so why not?"

Darius responded with a fake punch to his gut.

Soon, everyone was filing onto the patio from either inside the house, or down on the beach to fix their plates. Rashad and Darius had prepared massive amounts of grilled chicken, steaks, burgers and ribs, while the women had contributed tossed salad, baked beans, macaroni salad and a bevy of other sides. Lina was among the people in line, and she threw him a sexy wink as she descended the stairs with her food.

Once Rashad was finally released from his grill duty, he fixed himself a plate, grabbed a soda from one of the three ice-filled coolers and went off in search of Lina.

He found her on the beach, sitting on the big blanket she'd brought. Her spot was somewhat secluded, away from the house but still in the shadow cast by the structure. Mere feet away from where she reclined with her plate, the water lapped against the shore.

He set his plate on the blanket, then sat down next to her. "Enjoying the baby shower?"

"It's the most fun I've ever had at a baby shower. They should all be like this." She lifted her can of grape soda to her mouth and took a sip.

They ate in congenial silence. While she watched the tide rolling in and out, he watched her. He thought back on Darius's words on the patio, about not waiting too long to make things official with her. The breeze wafting over the water played through her hair, lifting her curls away from her face. God help him, even her chewing mesmerized him. In that moment, he knew his best friend was right. What would be the purpose of waiting to start a life with her when he knew he didn't want to imagine a life without her?

As if she'd just noticed him staring at her, she put down her fork and turned to face him. "Rashad? What is it?"

"You know I don't ever want to spend another day of my life without you, right?"

Her face lit up with a sweet smile, and she lay a soft hand against his jaw. "Don't worry. You won't have to."

He rewarded her with a series of brief kisses on

the lips. Pulling away before his desire for her super-seded his sense of propriety, he looked into her spar-kling brown eyes. "I want to make this thing official with you, baby."

A blush crept into her cheeks. "I know what you're getting at, and you know I'm down, but..."

"But?" He felt his eyebrow hitch, wondering what could be making her hesitant after all they'd been through to reach this point.

"There is something that needs to happen first, be-fore I can make this commitment to you. Because once I do, I'm in this thing with you for life."

He drew her into his arms, with her back resting against his chest. "That's just the way I want it. And if you mean you want me to ask your mother's permis-sion, I had already planned to do that."

"That's not what I meant, but I definitely approve." She rested her head on his shoulder. "I mean, there's something I need to handle on my own. Once I do, I'll be ready to do this the right way."

He wasn't sure what she meant, but he trusted her. "Whatever you need."

"Thank you." She settled back into his embrace, and as dusk came on, the two of them enjoyed the sight and sounds of the ocean together.

## Chapter 18

Pulling her car around the circular driveway in front of Eve and Darius's house, Lina honked her horn. She'd called her best friend the previous day, and asked her to accompany her to a "celebration." Now, as she idled the engine and waited for Eve to come outside, Lina glanced into the backseat of her car at the supplies she'd brought. It was the second week of July, and the rising heat of summer had begun in earnest. Before coming to pick Eve up, she'd assembled everything she would need: a bottle of sparkling grape juice, two plastic champagne flutes, an envelope and a bright red balloon filled with helium.

Within a few minutes Eve appeared at the door. When Eve had asked Lina how she should dress for this mysterious celebration, Lina had told her to dress comfortably. Eve wore a sky-blue halter-neck maxi dress in a soft fabric that billowed around her growing stomach as it flowed to her feet. Lina thought that funny, since she was wearing a dress almost the same color, but hers was strapless and shorter. Their similar taste in clothing was part of what made them such good friends.

Darius waved to Lina as he appeared behind his wife, draping his arms around her waist. Lina waved back and watched the two of them standing in the doorway, saying goodbye. Witnessing the way he placed a loving hand on the small swell of Eve's stomach, and the gentle way he kissed her, Lina couldn't help smiling at them. Seeing her friend so happy and in love gave her a wonderful feeling inside, and that joy only increased now that she had the same kind of happiness in her own life.

She was still grinning when Eve finally descended the stone steps and opened the passenger side door. Sliding into the seat, Eve took one look at her face and said, "What?"

"Girl, come on. You two are so damn sweet you make my teeth hurt." Lina gave her a playful pat on the shoulder and waited while she buckled herself into the seat.

"Mmm-hmm. Pretty soon, you and Rashad are gonna be the same way. Hell, based on what I saw at the baby shower, you're at least halfway there."

Lina giggled as she put the car in gear and rounded the driveway, headed back toward the main road. "How are you feeling? Any morning sickness?"

"A little, but so far, it's not too bad. As long as I re-member to have saltines and a glass of water before I get out of bed in the morning, I do all right." She placed her palms on her stomach.

"You're starting to get a little baby bump. It's cute."

Eve scoffed. "Yeah, you say that now. But in a few months I'll probably be looking like a beached whale."

Stopped at a red light, Lina looked at her friend's face. "You're only a few months in, don't worry about gaining weight. I've never known you to be concerned about that kind of thing before."

Shifting in the seat, Eve nodded. "I'm telling you, it's the hormones. I'm crying at the drop of a hat, laugh-ing hysterically at things that aren't all that funny. Hopefully things will even out in the next trimester."

"Hopefully." Lina hit the gas when the light turned green. She was sympathetic to Eve's plight, especially since she hoped to one day experience motherhood. "Whatever happens, you know I'll be there for you, girl."

"I wouldn't expect any less from the baby's god-mother. Say, where are we going, anyway?" Eve peered out the window at the passing scenery.

"Marshall Park."

Eve all but shouted her response. "What?"

"We're going to Marshall Park."

"Why in the world would you want to go where Warren proposed to you? I thought you said you never wanted to set foot over there again?"

Lina could sense her friend's trepidation. "Calm

down. I'm going over there of my own free will because there's something I need to do."

"I thought we were going to a party."

"I didn't say a 'party,' I said a 'celebration.' There's a difference."

Eve folded her arms over her chest, and sat back in the seat. "If you say so."

Lina shook her head, turning the wheel to direct the car into the parking lot at Marshall Park. As one of the city's older parks, Marshall had opened back in the '70s. The dedication of the land came thirty years after James B. Marshall, the park's namesake, had served as city manager of Charlotte. It was a beautiful place, with rolling green lawns, a walking trail, picturesque views of Queen City's skyline and a small lake. It was near that lake, just over a decade ago, where Warren had asked Lina to marry him.

She pulled into an empty spot and shut off the engine. She opened her door and climbed out, noting Eve's hesitation. Eve continued to sit there, gawking at Lina while she took the balloon, the envelope and the bag with the grape juice and glasses from the backseat.

Chuckling to herself, Lina walked around and opened the passenger side door. "Eve, are you just going to sit in the car?"

Eve side-eyed her. "What exactly are we doing here, Lina?"

"You trust me, right?"

Eve responded with a slow nod.

Lina extended her hand and helped her best friend up from the seat. Closing the door behind her, Eve accepted the balloon from Lina and followed her across the grassy landscape.

As they walked toward the lake, Lina took in the scenery. The view of the city was just as lovely as she remembered, even though she hadn't been there in years. A few ducks and geese skated along the glassy surface of the water, leaving ripples in their wake. When she reached the spot near the water's edge, where she'd stood with Warren many years ago, she stopped.

She inhaled a few deep breaths of sweet, fresh air.

Behind her, Eve stood, clutching the balloon string. "What are we doing here, Lina?"

"You're right, I did say I never wanted to come here again. The memories were too painful. The night Warren proposed to me here, I thought it meant we'd be together forever. Time showed me who he really was, though."

Silently, Eve stepped closer behind her and draped an arm around her shoulder. "I'm here for you, girl."

"I know, and I'm glad, because I want you to see this." Lina opened the envelope she'd brought with her and showed Eve what was inside.

Eve gasped. "I didn't know you still had your wedding band."

She nodded. "Yeah. I won it in the divorce settlement, along with the house, one of the cars and alimony. Sold the house and the car and bought my new place, but never did get rid of this damn ring."

Eve gave her shoulder a squeeze.

"I've been holding on to it, and the pain Warren caused me, for too long. At first I thought I'd go talk to him, but I realized that would be pointless. I don't want to talk to him and, besides, this isn't about him. It's about me."

"Amen. I think I finally figured out what we're doing here." She held out the balloon string.

Lina removed the band from the envelope. It wasn't anything fancy, just a thin, polished circle of yellow gold. It only took her a few seconds to tie the end of the balloon string around it. Once it was secure, she took the balloon from Eve.

"Time to let it go." Lina took a deep breath, and released her hold on the string.

The balloon caught an air current immediately and began moving away from them as it rose. Lina watched it float away, taking with it her feelings of resentment and mistrust, and the last thing she had that tied her to Warren. She might never be able to forget what he did to her, but she would forgive him. Now that Rashad had come into her life, she refused to let the baggage of a long-dead relationship keep her from the happiness she needed and deserved.

She stood on the bank of the lake, arm in arm with Eve, and watched the balloon rise until it was out of sight. Once it was gone, she felt a certain lightness descend upon her, and a smile spread across her face.

Her arm still linked with Eve's, the two of them strolled toward a bench for a celebratory drink.

Rashad closed his hand around Lina's and gave it a squeeze. They were sitting on the sofa in the modest living room of her mother's house. Carla, ever the gracious hostess, was currently busy banging around in the kitchen. She'd gone in there a few moments ago to get them something to drink.

He and Lina sat so close together that their thighs were touching, and he let his gaze sweep over the tempting length of her legs, bared by the blue dress she wore. As his watchful eyes traveled up to meet hers, he noticed the serene smile on her face. He still didn't know what she'd done today, and at this point it didn't much matter to him. Her assurance that she was ready, along with the peace that seemed to be radiating from her, were enough for him.

He trusted her, so there was no need to question her every move. And he felt they'd finally reached the point in their relationship where she trusted him, as well. Now there was nothing to hold them back from the future he dreamed of sharing with her. He could imagine waking up to her beautiful smile every day, holding her in his arms every night, and some day, seeing her belly swell with his growing child. The hand he held in his at that very moment was the one he wanted to hold until he drew his last breath. Of that, he was sure.

Carla walked in carrying a small silver tray that held three glasses of iced tea. Once everybody had a glass, she finally sat down. "I'm so glad you all stopped by to see me."

"You know I come by whenever I have free time, Mama." Lina sipped from her glass.

"Thanks for having me, Mrs. Smith." Rashad gave a respectful nod in her direction.

"None of that Mrs. Smith nonsense. Call me Carla."

Rashad looked into Lina's smiling eyes, then turned his attention to her mother. "Actually, Carla, I have a question I wanted to ask you."

The older woman moved to the edge of her seat on the flowered armchair. "Sure, honey, what do you want to ask?"

"I wanted to seek your blessing in asking Lina to be my wife."

Immediately, Carla's face broke into a broad grin. "Sure enough! Amen. Son, you have my blessing. I haven't seen my baby this happy in years."

He squeezed Lina's hand again, but kept his attention on her mother. "Thank you."

"Lord, this is wonderful. You're a good man, Rashad, and I know her daddy would approve, as well." Carla clasped her hands together, an expression of sheer delight on her face.

He was glad to finally have Carla's blessing, because the ring he'd purchased for Lina was practically burning a hole in his pocket. He reached into his slacks now for the small black box.

Lina clasped both hands over her mouth as he knelt at her feet.

"Now that you've done what you needed to do, and your mother's on board, I don't want to wait any longer to ask you this. Lina Dianne Smith, will you be my wife?"

Tears sprang to her eyes as she nodded furiously. "Yes, Rashad. Yes."

He grasped her trembling hand and carefully slipped the square cut solitaire onto her finger. The next thing he knew, she was on the floor with him, kissing him with fervor.

He held back, aware of her mother sitting behind them. When Lina pulled away, his heart swelled at the sight of her happiness. She was still crying, smiling and staring at the ring. In that moment, he knew he'd gotten it right.

After he'd shared hugs with his soon-to-be mother-in-law, he watched Lina grab her smartphone and disappear out the front door, presumably to call everyone she knew and spread the news. Once his fiancée was safely out of earshot, he turned to Carla.

She eyed him suspiciously. "Your face says you're plotting something. What is it?"

He smiled, gave her shoulder a squeeze. "Carla, I think I've got the perfect wedding present in mind for Lina, but I want it to be a surprise. I'll need your help to put it together. What do you say?"

Her expression morphing back into delight, Carla nodded. "I say, what do you need me to do?"

He quickly leaned down and whispered his plan into her ear.

When he straightened, he saw the tears standing in Carla's eyes.

Her voice shaking with emotion, she said, "My Lord. That's the most wonderful gift you could give her, and me. Thank you, son. Thank you for being so thoughtful."

She gripped him in a tight hug, which he returned. Knowing Carla approved of his intention, and seeing how touched she was by the gesture he planned to make, filled him with a sense of pride. Now all that was left to do was to notify his family of his upcoming nuptials. Since Lina was still standing on the front porch yammering on her phone, he could safely assume she'd tell everybody in her contact list.

He turned toward the front window, his eyes landing on her back as she stood outside, talking and flailing. Even from this distance, her excitement and happiness were palpable. He loved her, and he loved being the one who filled her with joy. Staring at the profile of his future wife, he felt his heart somersault in his chest. Everything they'd gone through to reach this point had been totally worth it.

Because soon, Lina would be his, for keeps.

# Chapter 19

*Six Weeks Later*

With her mimosa in hand, Lina flopped down onto Eve's white leather sofa and sighed with contentment. In several hours, she would become Mrs. Rashad MacRae. When she and Rashad had sat down to plan the wedding, they'd both agreed on two things: there was no need to drag out the engagement, and the ceremony should be small, classy and simple.

The day had dawned a beautifully sunny Saturday morning, the first of September As Lina sipped her drink and looked out the picture window at the mani-cured lawns of Eve's property, she felt the happiness of the day fill her soul. Eve's idea to have a celebratory brunch on her wedding day, since there hadn't been time for a bridal shower, had been nothing short of brilliant. She and her four closest girlfriends had enjoyed a sumptuous catered breakfast buffet, manicures and pedicures, and were now relaxing around Eve's palatial house as the afternoon began.

Eve strolled in, still wearing her white Serenity Spa bathrobe and a headful of hot rollers. "So, how are you enjoying your wedding day so far, girl?"

"I'm finding it quite lovely, thank you. Where are the rest of the girls?"

"Fiona's on her way, you know she's always late. Ophelia and Denise are with the hairdresser in one of the bedrooms upstairs."

Lina drained her glass and set it down. "Okay, I think that's going to be my one and only mimosa. I'd like to be upright and coherent enough to say my vows."

Eve giggled. "No worries. I made the drinks heavy on orange juice, with just a drop of vodka. All except mine, which was all juice." She stuck her lips out in a mock pout as she rubbed her growing stomach.

"I salute your sacrifice. Keep up the good work, because I expect you to be very cautious about your diet while you're baking my little 'god-bun.'" Lina gave Eve's stomach a loving pat.

Denise walked in then. She still wore her robe as well, but her Afro was done, having been blown out and neatly shaped by the hairdresser. "O's still in the chair. Takes a lot of work to tame those locks."

Lina sank back into the cushions and sighed. "I can't

believe this day is finally here. I just hope Rashad will like my gift."

Eve sat down on the arm of the sofa. "I don't see why he wouldn't love it. I bet he'll be thanking you all night long, girl." She gave an exaggerated wink.

Shaking her head, Lina chuckled. Securing Rashad's wedding gift on such short notice had not been an easy feat. If he loved it as much as she hoped he would, his reaction would be well worth the effort she'd put in.

Denise's brow knit with confusion. "Okay, spill it. What exactly did you get him?"

"You know how that piano reunited us, right? So I thought, since he took the high road and donated Monk's piano to the museum, I'd get him something else of Monk's to replace it."

"So, what did you get him?" Denise was literally on the edge of her seat.

Lina clasped her hands together. "Monk's son."

Denise's confused expression deepened. "What?"

"Thelonious Monk, Jr. I was able to get in contact with his rep, and he agreed to play at the ceremony. Rashad has no idea he's going to be there."

"Wow. Good one, sis." Denise fist-bumped her.

"He goes by TS Monk to cut down on confusion with his father, but he definitely inherited the musical talent. He's made a name for himself as a jazz performer. Some of the money I was going to spend on the piano went to pay his appearance fee, in the form of a donation to the Thelonious Monk Institute of Jazz. Money well spent."

Ophelia's voice called out from upstairs. "Lina, ain't it about time you got dressed, girl?"

Looking at the old grandfather clock in the corner of the den, Lina got up from her comfy seat. "O's right. It's already one o'clock, and I don't want to be late to my own wedding."

"It wouldn't be a good look," Eve cracked.

The three robe-clad women climbed the stairs to the second level of the house and entered the room Eve had set up for them to get ready. They passed the hairdresser on her way out, and Lina gave her a generous tip along with her thanks for making a house call.

Inside the guest bedroom, Ophelia sat on the edge of the bed, clipping garters to a pair of nude thigh highs. Ophelia's long, thin locks had been curled and pinned up on top of her head. On their entry, she straightened. "All right. Let's get you ready, Lina."

In keeping with the tone of the ceremony, Lina had eschewed a big poufy gown in favor of a cream-colored cocktail dress. After her girls laced her up into her bridal corset, she got into the dress on her own. Since she hated pantyhose, she didn't wear them. She stepped into three-inch satin pumps that matched her dress, and let Eve place the crystal-encrusted barrette she'd chosen in lieu of a veil in her curls.

Once the girls got into their soft yellow, one shouldered dresses, Lina gave her reflection a final check in the full-length mirror. The woman looking back at her was resplendent with happiness, abounding in love and fully ready to commit to the man who'd be waiting for her.

She turned to her girlfriends, her smile reflective of the happiness she felt inside. "Let's go, girls."

With sure, steady hands, Rashad gave his clothes one final adjustment. The ivory button-down shirt was properly tucked into the slacks of his navy suit. He carefully tied the Windsor knot of the navy-and-yellow-striped tie around his neck, then shrugged into his sport coat.

He and his boys were in a spare room at the Afro American Arts Museum, hanging around in the final moments before the ceremony. Darius, Marco and Ken, all similarly dressed, were currently clowning around behind him. He chose to ignore their horseplay in favor of keeping his mind occupied with thoughts of the beautiful woman who would soon become his wife.

Tandy, the museum staffer who'd been placed in charge of coordinating the ceremony, poked her head into the room. "Mr. MacRae, this package was left on Monk's piano, addressed to you."

He strode over to the door, took the large padded envelope she held out. "Thank you."

"We're ready for you guys, whenever you're ready."

She disappeared, and he inspected the envelope. His name was printed on it in block letters, but there was no clue as to who might have left it.

Turning it over, he pulled off the tape securing the flap, then reached inside. When he pulled out the wooden frame and saw what was in it, his breath caught.

"Guys, come look at this."

Darius, Marco and Ken came over, and soon they were all staring in wide-eyed awe.

Inside the frame was an aged piece of sheet music. The composition was "'Round Midnight," and the lyrics were handwritten in the margins. At the bottom of the last staff were the initials T.S.M. When Rashad turned the frame over, he saw a yellow sticky note attached to the back of the frame. It read,

Love is the music of the soul. May your harmonies be ever beautiful. The Music Man.

"That's just like the picture of the Duke that was left on my porch. It's got to be the same person." Darius's brow furrowed.

Rashad shook his head in amazement. "I'm guessing you still don't know who he is?"

Darius' shrug told him that The Music Man's identity was still a mystery.

"We'll figure it out eventually, but right now, there is the matter of you getting married." Marco tapped his gold wristwatch.

Rashad knew his friend was right, so he slid the framed sheet music back into the envelope and tucked it beneath his arm. "Let's go."

Quietly, the four of them filed out of the room and down the hallway toward the main gallery, where the wedding would take place.

Their family members and friends were already seated and carrying on muted conversations. Rashad smiled at the sight of his maternal grandmother, Annmarie, who'd come all the way from Trinidad to witness his marriage.

Rashad could hear the strains of someone playing a piano. He'd heard the music from the hall, and now that they were in the room, the sound grew louder. Though the chairs and the altar had been set up around Monk's piano as he and Lina requested, the music was coming from elsewhere. Letting his eyes scan the room, he searched to see who was playing.

And nearly fell over when he saw TS Monk tickling the keys of an upright piano set off to the side of the main exhibit.

A smile spread across his face, and he broke ranks with his boys to walk over to the piano.

Thelonious Jr. stopped playing long enough to stand and shake hands with him. "You must be Rashad. Congratulations, man."

"Wow. Mr. Monk. Thank you so much for coming. I'm a big fan, of both you and your father."

"I appreciate that. And please, call me TS."

He couldn't remember ever being this star-struck, so he took a deep breath to steady his voice before he asked the obvious question. "I'm honored that you came, but I have to ask. What are you doing here?"

"Your fiancée told me how much my father's music meant to you. And, she made a very generous donation to my father's foundation." TS went back to playing the piano, his manner as casual as could be.

He wanted to show TS the sheet music, but knew time was running short. Aside from that, it seemed pretty unlikely TS Monk was the music man. That wouldn't make sense considering Darius's gift.

Still shocked and utterly thrilled, Rashad walked back across the room and took his appointed place. All the while, he couldn't help thinking what a remarkably thoughtful woman Lina was, and how blessed he felt to be marrying her.

Darius elbowed him. "Dude, fix your face. Your jaw's hanging wide-open."

Shaking his head, Rashad did as he was told.

The judge who would serve as officiant took his place next to Rashad, and with the change in the music, everyone directed their eyes toward the door.

Lina's girlfriends processed in and took their places.

When Lina stepped into the room, the sight of her took his breath away. The pearl-encrusted dress left the length of her honey-brown legs exposed to his eyes, but she remained as classy and elegant as the occasion called for. The look in her eyes, however, told her she had intentions for him that were anything but proper.

She finally reached him and passed her bouquet to Eve, then joined hands with him. The vows were said, promises exchanged, and a few minutes later, Rashad locked lips with his new wife. Mindful of the friends and family present, he kept the kiss chaste. In his mind, he knew there would be plenty of time to unleash the full measure of his passion for her later, in private.

The ceremony ended, and everyone remained in the main gallery as the staff reconfigured the room. Chairs were moved aside to make room for dancing, and tables were moved into place. TS came over to congratulate them again before he left, and was gracious enough to autograph a wedding program as a keepsake.

A string trio came in and quickly set up, soon filling the space with music once again. Rashad was barely aware of any of the commotion because he had eyes only for Lina. They were standing in a corner of the room, embracing and stealing kisses.

He stroked his fingertips along the silken line of her jaw. "Thank you so much for getting TS Monk here, baby. I'm so amazed that you would even think of that."

Her responding smile was soft and affectionate. "You're welcome. Although you should know I'll expect a full and proper thank-you this evening."

Leaning down near her ear, he whispered to her a few of the naughty things he planned to do to show his gratitude, while she giggled and turned red.

Someone cleared their throat, and he jerked his head away from the crook of her neck.

Standing in front of them, aided by a carved mahogany cane, was his grandmother, Annmarie. In her thick island accent, she admonished, "Save some for da hotel, before ya set da drapes afire."

Rashad couldn't help laughing as he leaned over and took his little firecracker into his arms for a hug. "Grandma, I'm so glad you could come. How have you been doing?"

"Eighty-six years on dis good earth, and I'm feeling like a teenager." She gave him a kiss on the cheek, then turned to Lina. "And you, come here to me. You done walked in my dreams till I feel I know ya."

Looking somewhat confused, Lina hugged Annmarie.

"I'm so happy to meet you, Mrs. Callahan, but I'm afraid I don't know what you mean."

"For many months, I dreamed of you. Same dream over and over again. I told Rashad of dis. In my dream, I walk pon the shore, and you wash up there, like a mermaid. Then I watch Rashad come der, scoop you up in his arms and carry you away."

Lina turned her questioning gaze on him.

He shrugged. "She knows things. Don't ask me how."

Shaking her head, Lina grasped Annmarie's hand. "I don't know how you knew, either, but I'm glad you were right."

Annmarie chuckled. "I'm always right, honey. Didn't live this long by being dense."

Watching the two of them, he felt his heart swell with love. Knowing that his mother, his sister and now his grandmother all loved Lina delighted him.

As the evening went on, the time finally came for them to cut the small cake. After that, he raised his glass to his new bride, happy to finally be able to announce his wedding gift to her.

"My wife has given me a priceless experience of meeting someone I truly admire, and I only hope my gift touches her the way her thoughtfulness did to me. Ladies and gentleman, I'm proud to announce that I've given an endowment to the Afro-American Museum in the amount of three hundred thousand dollars." He paused, locked eyes with Lina. "This gift is given in the name and memory of Mr. Bradford Smith."

Her hand flew to her mouth, and tears welled up in her eyes, spilling onto her cheeks. "Oh, Rashad."

As soon as the emotion-filled words left her mouth, he leaned down to kiss her. "Welcome to life with me, baby. I plan on spending the rest of my life making you feel this way."

She wrapped her arms around his neck and leaned up to be kissed again. Cheers erupted in the room as they shared a kiss as sweet and potent as the joy of their special day.

And later that night, when he carried her over the threshold of their honeymoon suite, he showed her just how grateful he was to have her in his life.

# *Epilogue*

Lina pressed her free hand over the crown of her wide-brimmed sun hat to keep the strong ocean breeze from blowing it away. Her other hand was nestled into Rashad's as the two of them strolled along a bustling street near the center of town.

"It's really beautiful here, Rashad." This was her first time visiting the island of Trinidad, and she'd been enjoying every moment of it. Their days were spent wandering the streets of Toco, where his mother had been born and his grandmother still lived. The town sat on the far northeastern corner of the island, boasting rocky cliffs and spectacular views of the Caribbean Sea.

"I'm glad you like it. Grandma has been on me about not visiting her enough, so we'll be coming here often."

She quieted, taking in more of the scenery. Today's sojourn had brought them to Galera Point. According to Rashad, the famed lighthouse was a significant local landmark.

He pointed up to the lighthouse now. "The lighthouse was built in 1897, and it's been here ever since. There was some talk of making the area a national park, but I don't know if that idea ever got off the ground."

She looked up at the tall, whitewashed structure. The bright red door stood as a stark contrast to the rest of its exterior, and she could see the Spanish influence in its architecture.

They moved down to the park surrounding the structure, and took a seat on a wooden bench overlooking the water. The sparkling blue surface reflected the bright sunshine, and as she snuggled close to her husband, she knew she'd have no qualms about visiting this island sanctuary as often as he wanted.

"Thanks for bringing me here." She placed her hand along his jaw.

Looking into her eyes, he smiled. "Thanks for coming into my life, baby."

She leaned up for his kiss. And as their lips touched, all the love they shared flowed between them, just as the sea flowed to the shore.

\* \* \* \* \*

*The sweetest merger of all…*

# YAHRAH ST. JOHN

*Cappuccino Kisses*

Mariah Drayson is set to run the Seattle branch of her family's legendary patisserie. And when high-end coffee importer Everett Myers joins forces with her, he knows they're a winning team. But is Mariah prepared to reveal the secret that could cost her a future with Everett?

The Draysons  Sprinkled with Love

*Available June 2016!*

**"This book has it all: passion, anger, deception, lust, family and love."**
—*RT Book Reviews* on *DELICIOUS DESTINY*

*Fire and ice...*

# ZURI DAY

*Sapphire* **ATTRACTION**

Real estate mogul Ike Drake Jr. likes women who are reliable. Quinn Taylor is unpredictable. Simple chemistry won't be enough to bridge the gap between them. It'll take the kind of trust that requires putting your heart on the line to secure a priceless future...

*The Drakes of California*

*Available June 2016!*

KPZD455

# Hearts in harmony?

## CANDACE SHAW

KIMANI™ ROMANCE

*His*
**LOVING**
*Caress*

★★★
CHASING LOVE

**CANDACE SHAW**

*His*
**LOVING**
*Caress*

Elle Lauren's stunning wedding gowns give brides the happily-ever-after she didn't have. Ignoring her childhood sweetheart's long-distance apologies has been easy, but seeing Braxton Chase once more stirs deep longings. Can he convince her to trust the sweet melody of their lost love once again?

★★★
CHASING LOVE

*Available June 2016!*

**HARLEQUIN®**
™ www.Harlequin.com

KPCS454

# REQUEST YOUR FREE BOOKS!

## 2 FREE NOVELS
## PLUS 2 FREE GIFTS!

**KIMANI**
**ROMANCE**
™

## Love's ultimate destination!

KROM15

"Long time."

Camille was speechless. She'd heard him speak but
was still so much in shock that nothing came out except
for an embarrassing hiccup courtesy of the wine. And
then she took him in. His height, strong facial features,
the shaved head and slight beard, the smoothness of his
caramel skin, and the very manly scent emanating from
his direction made her drift closer to him.

The man was sexy and the sight of him made her libido
spring to life.

Camille's mouth opened and closed until finally she took a step back and said, "Why are you here, Remi?" Her voice trembled and she got angry with herself for becoming a blubbering idiot at the mere sight of her former sweetheart.

"That should be obvious. I came here to see you, Camille."

"You wha… Why? I don't unders—"

He didn't wait for her to finish whatever it was she was going to say. He closed the distance between them and didn't hesitate to place his large, warm hands on either side of her neck using the pads of his thumbs to gently stroke her cheeks as if coaxing her to comply with his unspoken demand.

Shock, lust, confusion and longing snaked its way to every crevice of Camille's body. The overwhelming sensations made her dizzy. She was so busy trying to figure out what was going on that she had not even realized that it was already happening. His lips had found hers and he indulged in helping her remember times past.

When she started to respond with soft moans, his fingers curled into the hair at the nape of her neck. Remi pulled back, but only a fraction, leaving their lips achingly close…

*Don't miss RETURN TO PASSION*
*by Carla Buchanan, available July 2016*
*wherever Harlequin® Kimani Romance™*
*books and ebooks are sold.*